INSIDE THE PENALTY BOX

S.L. STERLING

Inside the Penalty Box

by

S.L. Sterling

©2024

Inside the Penalty Box

ISBN: 978-1-989566-69-5

Paperback ISBN: 978-1-989566-82-4

Harcover ISBN: 978-1-989566-83-1

Editor: Brandi Aquino, Editing Done Write

Cover Design: Thunderstruck Cover Design

I kept my nose clean. Bad publicity was the last thing you wanted, and I'd had my share since my last breakup went public. We'd also just lost our last five games.

The boys and I decided to head to the islands for a little R&R. I'd never been so happy for a break. That was where I saw her. She didn't seem to recognize me, which made it better, so I made my move. We didn't exchange names or numbers. We shared one carefree night, that was all I wanted and that was all it was supposed to be.

A few months later, regret from that night had almost eaten away at me. I hadn't been able to get her out of my mind. I wouldn't say I fell in love with her, or maybe I did. All I knew was that night was the closest I'd ever come to insta-love and I wanted more but we'd had our fun. Yet, I was still mentally kicking myself for at least not getting her name.

We're about to head into the playoffs when I return home and that is when the universe decides to bring us back together in one of the worst places ever. Only this time won't be like the last, I decide I won't let her slip through my fingers. This time, I've promised myself nothing, and all bets are off.

Chapter 1

Aurora

SINCE I WAS A LITTLE GIRL, I idolized my mother. To me, she always seemed to be free as a bird, something I wanted to be when I grew up. Nothing ever seemed to bother her. She never seemed to be stressed or anxious, unlike me. Over the years, she had her share of boyfriends. She'd also had her share of husbands—three in the last eight years. Each one of them ended on an unpleasant note, but she was resilient, and within weeks, my mother was usually back out there on the dating scene.

When I'd ask her if we'd ever have a father that stayed around again, she'd smile and say, "Aurora, life is to be lived. To take chances, to have fun. That is what I am doing, having fun. You'll understand one day."

Walker, my brother, and I often wondered if she had always been this way, especially when our father was alive. He passed away when I was only two, so I never really got to know him. Walker, who is a couple of years older than me, barely even remembered him. Mom told us stories about him, and it seemed like they'd had a rather normal marriage. In her recollection, she'd tell us he was down-to-earth, something she was not, but that he kept her grounded, which she admitted she desperately needed. From what she told us, he rarely took chances, especially once we were in the picture, which drove her crazy. She told us she loved him immensely, but she also craved the wild and spontaneous life, and once he was gone, that was what she sought, regardless of how it affected Walker or me.

In some ways, I wanted that type of life for myself, to have fun and to take chances, yet I craved stability, probably because it was something I never had. My mother wasn't around much, and when she was, she didn't want to be known as Mom, but as Penelope. She said it made her feel younger. In some ways, I almost felt that we didn't have a mother; we had a best friend instead.

My friends would laugh when I'd tell them I

wanted to be like my mother. When I'd ask why they were laughing, they'd tell me it was because I was the exact opposite of her, and they looked forward to the day that I actually took a chance on anything.

I'll admit, loosening up was hard for me. As much as I craved that same freedom my mother had, I craved structure as well. I took school seriously, focusing on passing every class I had with a high mark. I'd also dated the same guy for the past three years, and my life nearly ended when he broke it off with me. To be honest, I'd cried and moped around in bed for months afterward. Something I'd never seen my mother do. In fact, after her last breakup, she was onto the next man before the night had ended.

My brother was exactly like her, or perhaps he was more like the men she brought home. He was a player, and he'd learned from the best, so you couldn't fault him. He'd watched my mother, and he'd idolized most of the men she'd brought home, and he treated women exactly how these men had treated my mother and the way my mother treated men. When he got bored with his current fling, which never seemed to be longer than a week or two, if it even lasted that long, he'd drop them and move on to the next girl, who was in the shadows waiting.

These differences and flaws had led us both to where we stood right now—the Vancouver airport, together with bags in hand, going on two very separate paths.

"I'll see you in a few months," Walker said as he wrapped his arms around me one last time.

I hugged him tight, wishing that he wasn't leaving me for such a long time. "Just be careful. I need you to come home. I don't think I can handle Mom all on my own," I whispered, sniffling and wiping tears from my eyes.

"What on earth are you crying for? I'll be home before you know it. I'm not going off to war, you know, only to basic training," Walker said as he picked his duffel bag up off the floor and flung it over his shoulder. He headed through the door to board his plane.

Sniffling, I stood with my luggage, crying and waving as I watched him disappear. I blew my nose, wiped my eyes, and turned away, pulling my carry-on behind me, and headed toward my gate.

It was sheer luck Walker was leaving the same day I was flying to Mexico with the girls. It had been an impromptu decision for him to join the army. An uncomfortable decision for me since we had grown so close over the years. The army wasn't always his plan, but circumstances beyond his control had led him to this path, which conveniently happened right after we'd attended a year-end party at some schoolmate's house.

My best friend Lorelai had broken up with her boyfriend of five years. She was on a collision course to punish herself, and she went after Walker. I tried to persuade her not to, but she was insistent. My brother, being the asshole he is, took her upstairs and, in his words, screwed the ex-boyfriend right out of her head.

Once it was over, they came downstairs and, if it was possible, he tore her already broken heart into a million more tiny pieces. He looked her up and down, chuckled to himself, shook his head, ran his hand over the stubble on his chin and said, "Darlin, thanks for the evening, but I'm not the type of guy for you." Then he took his drink and disappeared into the crowd.

Twenty minutes later, she was crying on my shoulder, and when I saw my brother, I let him have it. He took off with a group of friends and got arrested for drinking and driving a few hours later. I'd hated him for hurting her that way. Lorelai was my best friend, and even though she claimed she was only looking for a fun time and nothing permanent, she at least deserved a guy who'd treat her with some form of respect.

The next couple of weeks, she moped around over my brother, but come the end of the summer, she finally agreed with me it had been a stupid idea to even entertain getting involved with him.

For a long time, I could still see the hurt and disappointment on her face. The part that pissed me off most was that, for a bit, every time someone would mention his name, she'd fight back tears. She did not know how lucky she was that he'd spared her heart and acted like an asshole, even if at the time it hadn't felt like it.

The end of summer came. Boyfriend number twelve (I think) had just left my mother. Walker was still doing his community sentence, and that was when he announced he was changing his life and joining the army.

I was still angry with him and trying to deal with how he'd treated my best friend when he told me. So, I did the most spontaneous thing I'd done in my life: forgave my brother instantly and agreed to be dragged away by my five best friends to an island for five nights. I had a goal in mind: to get over my breakup before I started my last semester of the sports therapy program, and to have one last get-together with my friends before we all went our separate ways.

So, here I was wandering through the airport, pulling my suitcase behind me. It was so busy I doubted I'd ever find my gate or my girls. Looking down at my boarding pass, I checked the number once more.

I let out a sigh, rounded a corner, and looked up, finally seeing a sign for my gate number up ahead.

Shoving my pass into my passport, I picked up my pace, then heard my name being called. I looked over my shoulder to see Lorelai running to catch up with me.

"Ready for fun in the sun?" I questioned, hoping that today she was in a better mood than she had been since the night of the party.

She smiled and nodded, but I could tell it wasn't her usual happiness. I knew she was still feeling crushed by my brother's actions and the breakup with her boyfriend. At least, I hoped that was the problem.

"Better put a smile on that face. You may meet the man of your dreams this week." I winked.

She groaned. "Look, I'm not looking for anything on this trip. After being dumped, then treated the way I was by your brother, I think I'll stay single. I pity the guy who tries anything with me next."

"Oh, no," I muttered, worried about my friend.

"Seriously, am I that bad?" Lorelai cried, meeting my eyes, tears lining them. "Is there something about me that men find repulsive?"

I'd been afraid that Walker's behaviour would have this effect, especially after she was just dumped. I was almost positive Lorelai would push all men away from her. She would not get over everything overnight.

"How many times do I need to tell you? It's not you, it's them. As for my brother, he's a mess.

Remember what his track record is," I said, gently banging her shoulder.

"I know, I just…can't forget the look on his face as he said those words to me. It was the same look that Hugo gave me when he broke it off with me."

"Please don't tell me you thought my brother would change because it was you?" I feared perhaps she had silently prayed for that. "Lorelai, I love you, but Walker has some serious growing up to do. He has had no male role model, aside from those disasters our mother has dated over the years. You've seen them. They aren't exactly model men. I mean, look at the last guy…leaving our mother for a woman on the internet or something."

"You're right. I don't know why I'm letting his reactions play any role in how I feel," she said, still looking defeated. "That night was nothing but a stupid mistake."

We walked in silence, then Lorelai turned to me.

"Are you still sure you want to be as free as her?"

I nodded. "I think that being like her would give me what I need to put my ex behind me."

"You do? You might end up like me. Whatever you do, just watch yourself, because that was what I thought. I don't want to see you getting hurt before we head off to school."

"I'll be careful. I know one thing: I will need a little courage to get there, to be as free as her."

Lorelai smirked. "Only a little? I'd say you'll need a lot. You aren't anything like her."

We both laughed, then she gave me a serious look.

"You don't need to do anything, you know. I think what would be best for you is just time. You were in a long relationship, and I know you well enough to know that you aren't the type to get over someone that quick or in that way. It may just confuse you more, just like it's done for me."

"I'm not confused," I said, feeling defensive.

"I beg to differ. The breakup came out of nowhere, and now you are seeking somewhere to divert your pain."

I nodded. "Yep, it came out of nowhere. It was like I walked into a wall. Pardon me if I just want to forget it all."

"Of course it did, and it doesn't help that he never even gave you an explanation! At least Hugo had a reason."

I shook my head. "No, Greg had a reason. He said he couldn't see us going any further."

"Poor excuse. I don't call a job in another city a reason. Hasn't he heard of long-distance relationships?"

I grew quiet, remembering exactly how I felt the

day that Greg announced he wanted to break things between us.

Lorelai was quiet for a moment. Then she looked at me. "I'm sorry he hurt you."

I shrugged. "It's not a big deal, really. It obviously was not meant to be. If we were, then, well, we wouldn't be here discussing this, would we?"

Lorelai shook her head. "I guess not."

"So, I'm reclaiming myself on this trip. I'm taking control of my life, just like my mother does. So, give me the courage to act like my mother. It works for her, so maybe, fingers crossed, it will work for me."

Lorelai let out a laugh. "You know what? You want courage? I'll give you courage. The first guy who looks in your direction, I'm going to tell him just to invite you back to his room and make you his."

I let out a loud laugh, while Lorelai kept a straight face. People glanced in our direction as they passed by.

"Okay, maybe not so forward."

"It's the only way to go," she said, looking at everyone.

"What are you doing? Here?" I gasped.

She nodded just as two guys about our age came walking toward us. Lorelai straightened up. "Hey, do either of you want to have one night of fun?" she asked them.

"Oh my god, stop," I whispered, pulling on her arm, but she shrugged me off.

"Hell yah, baby. What you got?" the one said as the other made eye contact with me.

"My friend here…" she said, grabbing my arm and trying to pull me in front of her.

"Oh my god, stop," I insisted, grabbing hold of Lorelai. "That's enough. They are going to think we are street women."

"Street women?" Lorelai frowned, shaking her head. "I'm only following your instructions…giving you courage." She giggled while the two guys stood there watching us.

"What the hell are you two laughing at?" I heard a familiar voice ask.

I looked to my left to see Hannah standing there smiling, clearly wondering what we were doing. Then I caught sight of Adalyn and Willow waving their arms in excitement at the gate. They all looked ready to party hard this weekend.

"Sorry, guys." Lorelai shrugged. "Our friends are waiting."

Both guys shook their heads and turned away from us as we ran toward the others.

"Fill us in. What were you doing back there?" Willow questioned as we sat down.

"Nothing," I muttered first.

"It was not nothing," Lorelai added. "I was trying to help Miss. Uptight here loosen up. Wait, no, give her courage…wait what am I supposed to do?" Lorelai questioned, looking over at me.

I shook my head. "Nevermind. This plan is a lost cause and probably going to be impossible," I muttered.

Chapter 2

Aurora - 4 Days Later

"I CAN'T BELIEVE it's one of our last nights," Willow cried as we made our way to the lobby for drinks. The days had flown by, and I'd barely accomplished getting a tan, never mind what I had set out to do.

"I'm starving and I'm in pain. I'm so sunburnt," Lorelai cried, looking down at her arms.

I glanced at her red skin on her shoulders and back. "I told you to wear the wetsuit," I muttered. "We were on a catamaran and snorkeling in the scorching sun all day and you refused to take the sunscreen from the guys who offered."

"I told you, I didn't want 'their hand' at putting it

on me. Plus, I'm positive I knew the one from somewhere."

"So, you could have taken it and given it to me. I would have put it on you," I bit out as I tried to apply a little more aloe as we walked.

"Who doesn't bring sunscreen?" Willow questioned.

"Girls who wear wetsuits," Hannah and Adalyn said in unison.

Lorelai glanced over at them and scowled. Looking at her burnt skin, I was glad it was one of our last nights here. From the looks of her, she wouldn't be taking part in much tomorrow.

"You know what I can't believe."

"What?" Willow asked.

"I can't believe that Aurora didn't act like her mother and drop to her knees for the guy who was eyeing her all day. He just looked too familiar to me, but I will agree he was hot and had an amazing body to go with it," Lorelai said, wincing in pain as we walked.

"You mean the one whose friend offered you sunblock that you wouldn't take?" I asked, looking at her.

"Yes, that one," she muttered.

"Same here, because damn, he was fine," Willow said, waving her hand in front of her face to cool herself. "I was actually looking forward to watching Aurora lose herself."

I'd be lying if I said Willow and Lorelai were lying. The guy was fine. Hell, he was more than fine, and so were the four guys he was with. However, I'd been too intimidated by him to even think about talking to him, never mind doing anything else.

Lorelai held true to her promise by trying to encourage me the entire afternoon. That was until the sunblock incident. That was when she finally gave up. The girls teased me the rest of the afternoon, while the guy gave me major glances for the rest of the day.

"How about a round of drinks?" Willow questioned as we approached a table in the lobby.

We all nodded just as our regular server approached our table, already carrying a tray full of shots and drinks. He placed a full glass down in front of each of us, smiling because he'd remembered our orders from the previous nights.

"Amazing!" Willow screamed, raising her hands above her head in excitement. "We have to get our friend here to loosen up so she can talk to the handsome man who's been eying her all day," she said, pointing to the four guys who'd been on our trip today.

"Oh god! He's here," I said, gripping Lorelai's arm, causing her to scream out in pain.

I wanted to kill Willow as the bartender looked at

the men she was pointing to and then looked my way. "Is that so…little shy, are you?" He chuckled.

Hannah reached for her shot of tequila and raised her glass in the air. "Ladies, come on, get those drinks and toss them back. This should help her loosen the hell up, Aurora. At least enough to go over and say hello and apologize for being so damn uptight."

I glared at the girls, becoming annoyed.

Adalyn and Willow picked theirs up and looked at Lorelai and me. We looked at one another and, feeling the pressure, picked ours up as well.

"To being single and free," Willow, Hannah, and Adalyn said in unison.

"And living without abandon like Aurora's mother!" Willow added, which she had done many nights this week.

The five of us chugged our tequila and then stuffed the lemon slices into our mouths and sucked. As I put my glass down, I caught sight of the guy who had been on the tour with us. Once again, he was staring back at me with those brilliant blue eyes of his against his tan skin as he ran his forefinger around the rim of his glass, brought his finger to his mouth, and sucked the salt off. I shyly smiled, which, of course, attracted all my friends' attention.

"Who are you smiling at?" Willow asked, looking over her shoulder toward the bar.

"No one," I mumbled, turning my attention back to what Hannah had been saying. There was no use. All eyes were on me.

"It's that guy," Adalyn said, turning back to me.

"And I said, it's no one. Now, continue with your story," I said, waiting for Hannah. Finally, she started talking again, keeping them all occupied.

"Another round of shots?" Willow yelled as soon as Hannah finished speaking.

I looked over at the bar once again while Willow tried to get the server's attention. The guy was still there, still staring at me. Once again, I shyly smiled in his direction. That was when he leaned over and whispered something to his friend, still not taking his eyes off me.

"No, no more for me," Lorelai replied, gripping my arm. "I'm done. I actually feel like I'm going to be sick."

"Yeah, Willow, any more and I think I'm going to be sick as well," Hannah cried, helping Lorelai up.

"Adalyn, Aurora?" Willow asked with a huff, waiting for us to answer.

Adalyn shook her head. "Willow, I'm going to have to detox my liver when I get home. I just can't." She placed her hand on her flat stomach.

Willow let out a laugh and turned to me. "Aurora?"

I shook my head. "Honestly, I think it's time we all turn in. It's been a long day. We've all been out in the sun, and I'm exhausted."

Lorelai, Adalyn, and Hannah all gathered their things as Willow turned to me. "You can't abandon me too. What about the fact you are supposed to be reclaiming your life?"

I glanced over to the bar to see the guy still staring. This time, a chill ran through me as I watched his eyes make their way down my body, drinking me in. I couldn't remember a single time in my life I'd seen a guy look at me that way. Then one of his friends handed him a drink and then leaned in and whispered something in his ear. He fist bumped the other two guys who were with them and they wandered off.

"Earth to Aurora?" Willow said, snapping her fingers in front of my face.

"No worries. I'll stay for one more drink, okay?"

"Yes!!!!!" Willow said as she took off toward the bar, leaving me at the table to say good night to the rest of the girls and watch them leave.

I turned and sat down while waiting for Willow to return when a server approached our table and set two shots along with two drinks on the table.

"Sorry, you must have the wrong table. My friend is at the bar getting our drinks."

The server smiled. "No, miss, this is the right table." He nodded toward the bar.

I looked up and over to see the guy who'd been staring at me for the past little while with one of his friends. They both raised their glasses to me and smiled just as Willow came back to the table and glanced over her shoulder.

She looked back at me and raised her eyebrows in jest. "Ohhh, this is it. This is where you lose all control and be like your idol," Willow said, her voice full of excitement.

I felt my cheeks heat and shook my head. "I don't think so."

"Oh, come on, live a little!" Willow cried. "He is fucking hot. Look at him, look at those broad shoulders, those amazing glass-blue eyes against that black hair, his fucking legs… Jesus even I'm getting wet at the thought of having him."

Was this really something my mother would do? Pick up a complete stranger at a bar and let the night take her where it may? Absolutely! However, my luck, I'd come home with some disease or worse, pregnant. I didn't have a care about what this guy wanted. Nor was I interested.

"I think my mission to reclaim myself is over," I muttered, shaking my head. "It was a stupid idea."

"At least drink the shot." She gently bumped me.

I gave her a look as we both picked up the shot and drank it back. The alcohol burned as it went down, bringing tears to my eyes, which I quickly blinked away. We placed the glasses down on the table and sat back down just as we heard a man clear his throat.

"Care to dance?"

We both looked up to see one of the guys who'd been with my admirer.

Willow gave a smile and looked at me as if I needed to decide for her, but I just shrugged.

"Well now, let's let this party begin, shall we?" She threw her head back and laughed, then followed the tall, muscular, dark-haired man to the dance floor.

I sat there shaking my head and laughing as I watched her dance with the guy. Willow always was a free spirit. If I'd not known, I'd say she was my mother's daughter and I'd been adopted. She was crazy. Once the second dance started, she came running over to me. "You may as well go to bed. I have a feeling it's going to be a late night." She giggled, hugged me, and ran back to continue dancing.

I sat there for a bit, watching them before getting up and gathering my things. I took one last look at my friend on the dance floor before walking away. She looked comfortable wrapped in his arms, and the second I saw them kiss, I knew she was fine. She appeared to be having a good time, and there were still many people around, so I made my way out of the lobby. Just as I reached the end of the walkway, I heard a throat clear. The guy from the bar stepped out from behind a pillar to my left, his blue eyes bright and twinkling.

"Your friend is out of control there." He chuckled, nodding in their direction.

"Yeah, well, what can I say? She's always up for a party," I said, glancing over my shoulder to see her grinding herself against the guy she was with.

"I see that." He chuckled, looking over at them. "And what about her friend?"

I softly smiled. "I'm not really that crazy."

"That's too bad. I could use some company tonight."

I felt my cheeks heat as I thought for a moment. I looked over at Willow to see she was still dancing with the guy.

"Well?" his deep voice asked.

A moment of unease passed through me, then I cleared my throat. "Sure, I'm—"

He held out his hand, stopping me from saying any more. "No names. Let's just have a night of fun."

Since I'd just broken up with Greg, and I really wasn't in any place to be looking for anything, I reminded myself that this was exactly something my mother would want, so I went with it.

"Okay, no names." I smiled.

He pushed himself off the railing he'd been leaning against and took my hand in his as we began walking.

"How did you enjoy today?" he questioned.

"Oh snorkeling? It was fun. What about you?"

"Not too bad. I'm not a huge fan of the ocean. I went more to appease my friends."

I smiled. "Same here."

"How long are you here for?"

"Five days, but we leave the day after tomorrow. It was a quick girls' trip before school starts. What about you?"

"We leave tomorrow morning."

"Ah, back to reality."

"Guess you could say that."

We stepped onto the beach, and I quickly slipped my shoes off. We continued to walk toward the water's edge, the cool sand beneath my feet. The water glistened as the moonlight danced over the gentle waves.

"It's beautiful," I whispered, stopping to stare.

"That it is," he whispered, bringing us to a stop.

When I finally looked at him, I noticed his heady eyes staring at me—a look that my ex rarely ever gave to me. He grabbed hold of both of my hands and gently pulled me forward until my body rested against his, then he slid his hands around my waist.

I swallowed hard as my body heated. He smelled good, a mixture of cologne, sweat, and sea air. His one hand locked on my waist, the other drifted slowly up to my cheek and slid into my hair. Our eyes met, and he leaned in, his lips gently grazing mine.

"I've been wanting to do that all day," he said in a throaty whisper.

I was so shocked I said nothing, and before I knew it, his lips met mine again.

Chapter 3

Aurora

MY BODY BECAME weak as his lips moved from mine to my ear, then to my neck and down to my bare shoulder while his hands explored my body. I could feel him straining through his pants as he pulled me closer. His hand lifted the edge of my skirt and his fingers danced up the back of my thigh and along my panty line.

As fire ran through my body, I placed my hands on his chest, pushing against him. I needed a second to breathe, anything other than physical contact because every nerve of my body was on fire, something I'd never experienced quite as intensely with anyone before.

I couldn't remember ever kissing someone who actually kissed the way he did. Greg never kissed me this way, and he'd never caused this much arousal in me, and here I'd thought he was going to be my forever.

"Something wrong?" he whispered in my ear, his breath tickling me, sending more waves through me.

"Give me a moment, just a second, to calm down," I said, breathing hard. My panties were soaked, my centre was throbbing, and I knew that if he slid my panties to the side and ran his fingers through my centre, I'd combust.

He chuckled, brought his hand to my cheek, and resumed kissing my neck, sucking my earlobe into his mouth and gently biting it between his teeth, not giving me even the smallest moment to calm down.

"How about we go back to your room," he whispered, his breath once again causing a shiver to go through my body. "We can get to know one another a little better," he whispered, sucking my earlobe between his lips.

A chill ran through me at the thought. I already knew that was exactly what I wanted, and then I remembered Lorelai.

"Um…my roommate…she is sleeping," I said,

closing my eyes and attempting to think of anything other than what he was doing so I could breathe.

"Come back to mine then," he said, his voice low and throaty while he pulled me gently toward the room buildings.

I closed my eyes. My heart was in my throat and my chest felt tight. My mouth was dry. I so wanted this…but this wasn't me. I swallowed hard. Could I do this for one night? Could I actually have a one-night stand with a guy I knew nothing about? I guess I could do this, get this urge to be spontaneous out of my system. Yes, I could be like my mother for only one night.

Minutes later, we were standing outside of his room. He fiddled with his keycard while I was pressed against the door as we kissed.

Finally, I heard the click of the lock and felt the door give way. He pinned me against the wall inside and shut the door. His hands ran over my body, down to the hem of my skirt. His rough fingers slid up the backs of my legs, finding my ass. He gripped me tight as he kissed me, his fingers finding their way into my panties and expertly sliding through my centre twice before he began tapping my clit, his lips still on mine, silencing my cries.

I gripped his shirt. I could feel myself losing control. "You've got to stop," I murmured breathlessly.

"Why?" he whispered, pulling his lips from mine and looking down into my eyes.

"Because…I'm going to…come," I whispered shyly.

"Come for me then," he whispered back, applying a little more pressure, now circling my clit over and over.

He held me tight in his arms as I felt my legs shake. In that moment, something came over me, and I brought my hands to his waist, pulling at the button on his pants, opening them.

"Fuck me," he hissed as I gripped his cock firmly and began stroking him.

His mouth crashed into mine hard as he pulled his hand from my panties, providing me with relief. Then he pulled my hand from his boxers, picked me up, and carried me over to the bed.

Dropping me onto the mattress, he reached behind his head and pulled his shirt off. My eyes travelled down his muscular chest to his eight-pack. I couldn't help but stare for a moment. I'd never been with a guy in such shape. When he met my eyes, I pulled my shirt off and dropped it to the floor as well. Then he dropped his pants and boxers, his cock springing free. I bit my bottom lip. Even his cock was amazing.

"Lift," he demanded as he took hold of my skirt and panties.

Excitement filled me. I swallowed hard as I did as I was told, and he pulled them off me, dropping them to the floor. Pushing me down on the bed, he knelt on the mattress and spread me open before him.

Moonlight poured through the sliding glass door enough that I could see his eyes wash over me. My stomach swirled with nerves, and as I watched his eyes roam my body, I was suddenly thankful the lights weren't on.

He took a moment to run his thumb through my wetness, then bent down to kiss me hard. He then leaned over, pulling a box off the night-table, and ripped open a condom wrapper, slid it on himself, and then lined himself up at my opening.

I could feel the intrusion starting and closed my eyes as I let out a small moan.

"Just relax," he said, inching his way a little more, practically torturing me as I felt the stretch.

I bit my bottom lip. I wanted to feel him. I wanted him to remove every memory of my ex from my brain.

"Relax," he soothed, bringing his thumb to my clit, rubbing me as he continued to slowly work his way inside me.

"That's it," he said breathlessly when I let out a loud moan as he gave me my wish, fully seating himself inside of me.

I closed my eyes as he started pumping into me.

Slow at first, then a little faster, a little harder. I could feel my orgasm building once again, and he reached down between us, his thumb finding my clit once again.

"I want you to come before me," he panted. "Girls always get to come before me."

I didn't know what it was about his voice saying those words that turned me on so much, but I felt my climax building fast. I gripped the sheets and went to place my hand on his to stop him from rubbing that sensitive bundle, but he took hold of my hands and held them above my head, pinning me to the mattress.

"Don't even think about it." He groaned. "You come before me, got it?"

Somewhere inside of me, I liked he was taking control and telling me how it was going to be. That differed from anything I'd ever experienced, so I did what he wanted.

I could feel the heat at the base of my spine build, and I tried to pull my hands from his one-handed grip, but it was useless. My legs went numb as my orgasm ripped through me, causing me to cry out. He let go of my hands and pumped hard into me, going deeper than before. His breathing changed, his muscles flexed, and he held me tight as he let go, eventually collapsing on me, breathing hard into the mattress.

I WOKE WITH A START. I didn't know how long I'd been asleep because I didn't remember coming back to my room. I didn't remember having that much to drink that I'd black out on my way back to my room, either. Regardless, I stretched and let out a breath, wondering what on earth had prompted that kind of dream. It had been so real, so vivid, it was as if it had actually happened. It was then I felt the bed move and someone let out a snore. Afraid to move, I glanced at the clock. A little after three. I quickly sat up, my body aching in spots it hadn't in a while, reminding me that the dream I'd had wasn't a dream but had really happened.

Panic filled my chest. Had I really had a one-night stand with a guy whose name I didn't know? Had I really acted just like my mother? Tears escaped my eyes. It was tequila, way too much tequila. That was what had happened, and Willow. She'd left me alone to be with that guy. If I knew her well, which I did, she'd probably set the entire thing up. The guy who distracted her and had sent me heading back to my room instead of sitting alone at a table was the entire reason I was in this mess. I tried to gather my thoughts as the man sleeping beside me let out a huge snore and rolled onto his stomach.

I had to get out of here before he woke. There was no way I could handle another round with him. I wasn't sure I wanted to either. He'd literally just blown my mind.

I slid from the bed, careful not to make any noise. I walked around the bed, bent down and grabbed my skirt, then my T-shirt. Stepping into the skirt, I threw my T-shirt over my head before realizing I didn't have my bra or my panties. I glanced around the room and spotted my bra slung over the TV, but my panties were nowhere to be found. Looking around the room again, I tried to think about when he'd taken them off but drew a blank as he shifted on the bed and stopped snoring. I needed to get out of here before he woke up.

As I made my way to the door, I began thinking of Lorelai. If she woke up and didn't find me in our room, she'd panic and probably call hotel security. I could just imagine her waking the others. It would be an embarrassing disaster that I hoped wouldn't happen.

I glanced at the door and held my breath as I waited for him to snore again. Surely, if I opened the door we'd come in, he'd wake. I glanced over to the large sliding door at the opposite end of the room and knew that was going to be my only chance.

As soon as he started snoring again, I grabbed my shoes, tiptoed to the other door, grabbing my bra on the way and slid the door open, slipping outside. I took one glance back to see if I could see my panties on the floor, but there was nothing. Then I looked over to make sure he was still asleep. He was, so I carefully and quietly shut the door.

The second the cool night air hit me, I started shaking. I walked as fast as I could to warm up, but I was frozen. Perhaps I wasn't cold and it was just anxiety. I couldn't believe what had happened, and as I made my way back to my room, I felt dirty. I wondered if this was what my mother felt like because if it was, it wasn't worth it.

My stomach turned more and more the closer I got to my room, and before I made it, I found myself bent over, throwing up in the bushes. I wiped my mouth with the back of my hand. What had I just done? This definitely wasn't something I'd ever do again, I thought to myself as I approached the door to my room, throwing up one more time in the bushes.

I tapped my keycard, stepped inside, slipped my shoes off, and tiptoed to my bed, quickly shedding my skirt. I crawled into bed, lay on my back and stared up at the ceiling, swallowing down the never-ending feeling of regret that was already settling in and vowed to myself never to mention the events of this night to anyone.

ONE THING I knew my mother never did was lose sleep over these types of things, which proved to me I'd probably made the worst mistake ever. I'd tossed and turned most of the night, the entire evening replaying over in my mind. I'd even thrown up one more time before the sun rose. When I decided I'd tortured myself enough, I got up early, took a hot shower, popped a motion sickness pill, and made my way down to the lobby bar to get a coffee before breakfast. I needed to clear my mind before the girls got to me, and the only way for me to do that was to be alone.

I sat at a table that seated five and sipped on my black coffee, a plate full of food in front of me. I'd already taken a walk on the beach, looking for little shells to divert my attention to anything but last night. Once the buffet opened, I wandered up and filled a plate full of fresh fruit and returned to the table, and now I sat looking out over the water. I was about to shove a piece of papaya into my mouth when I saw my friends approaching. Everyone looked well-rested, except Willow. She looked rough.

The four of them wandered over to the table and sat down.

"Didn't hear you come in last night. Or leave this morning," Lorelai said, shoving her beach bag under her chair before sitting down.

"Yeah, I was super quiet, didn't want to wake you," I lied, not wanting to give any hints to what had happened last night after I'd left Willow. However, she lowered her sunglasses and gave me a questioning look.

"Willow didn't come in until the wee hours of the morning." Adalyn giggled.

"Must have been a good night." Hannah laughed.

I looked at Willow, practically begging her not to say anything about me, only it did little good.

"It was, but I think you should all ask Aurora how her night was." She giggled, dropping her glasses back down to cover her bloodshot eyes.

All three girls looked at me, wondering what it was Willow was talking about. I looked at Willow, trying to hide the fact that I wanted to kill her for saying anything at all, then I turned to look at the girls.

"Well, come on, don't keep this a secret. We want all the details," Lorelai cried.

"Yeah, spill it." Hannah laughed. "It's probably way too good to keep to yourself."

"Was he tall, dark, and handsome? Did he slip you the tongue, or better yet…something else?" Adalyn questioned, resting her chin on her hand, her eyes full of curiosity.

I felt my cheeks flush at her suggestion because that was exactly what had happened, in exactly that order. I didn't want to tell them anything. The first thing they'd wonder was his name, and I didn't—huge tramp that I was—even know it. I mean, who the hell agrees to not exchange names? My stomach turned at the thought that I'd slept with a guy I knew nothing about. He could have had anything, I thought, beginning to panic only to remember he had worn a condom.

As I glanced around the table at my friends, I could see the questions in their eyes while I looked over at Willow, seriously ready to hurt her. How had she even seen me leave with him?

"Ask her what time she got in?" Willow giggled, knowing full well she was getting under my skin.

The three of them looked at me. "What time?" Lorelai asked, mild concern beginning to line her face.

Once again, I said nothing. I just glared at Willow, who sat there looking back at me, looking proud of herself, which made me wonder if she really hadn't orchestrated the entire thing.

"What is going on, Aurora?" Lorelai questioned. "Are you alright?"

Everyone was quiet as they waited for me to respond. Then Willow cleared her throat and leaned forward.

"I saw her pinned up against the wall outside that guy's room as he sucked on her neck around one in the morning." Willow laughed, looking at me over the frame of her sunglasses.

"You didn't!" Lorelai cried with excitement.

"Oh my god, you reclaimed yourself!" Adalyn cried as Hannah shook me with excitement.

"Tell us all about it!" Hannah exclaimed, while Lorelai looked at me with shock.

I buried my head in my hands, wishing I could hide from their eyes, but I couldn't. I was so ashamed and knew that this was why I didn't want to tell my friends. I couldn't imagine how my mother ever felt good about doing stuff like this.

"Girls, give her a moment to digest what has happened. Go get some food, you'll need it, because I have a feeling this story is going to be explosive!" Willow said, digging into her beach bag and pulling out some headache pills.

"You better introduce us to him later on," Adalyn said before standing up. "Ladies, shall we eat?"

"We need all the details," Lorelai added. "Leave nothing out."

"And she means nothing out." Hannah winked.

The three of them stood, but Willow stayed. "Go ahead," she said, dropping her glasses to cover her eyes once again. "I'm not hungry just yet."

We watched them walk away. I looked off toward the water. I had nothing to say to Willow. I was angry she'd do something like this to me. As soon as the others were out of earshot, Willow cleared her throat and put her hand on my arm.

"What?" I muttered, not turning to look at her.

"Aurora, there is no reason to be embarrassed at the fact you didn't get his name."

"How on earth do you know I didn't get his name?"

She shrugged. "I don't, but I sense something is different with you."

I looked over at her, wondering if she was just throwing things out there to see what would stick, or if she really did sense something different about me.

"Also, there isn't any shame in a one-night stand. Some of the best sex I've had in my brief life has been with one-night stands. I recommend everyone have at least one or two of them in their lifetime. The reason being is that there is no pressure if you don't know the person, nor any pressure because you never have to see them again if you don't want to. Makes for epic sex."

I felt my cheeks heat at the memory of last night. I didn't recall ever coming as hard as I did last night.

"See what I mean?" Willow whispered before she stood up and took off toward the other girls. Halfway across the room, she stopped and turned around, making her way back over to me. "Oh, and don't worry. I'm sorry if I put you on the spot. I didn't think it was that big of a deal. From now on, I promise I won't say anything about it to anyone. Now stop the blushing, own what happened, and eat your fruit."

Chapter 4

Aurora - 9 Months Later

I WAITED IMPATIENTLY, standing just outside the airport's departure area, watching people exit as I waited for my brother. His plane had come in late, which was making us late for our next stop, but I didn't care. I wasn't really all that excited about the next stop anyway. I let out a huff, sat down, and checked the time on my watch. When I looked up, I finally spotted Walker, his large green duffel bag flung over his shoulder, looking over the crowd for me.

I stood up, waving my hand in the air and smiling. This was the longest we'd ever been apart, and I'd missed him a lot. I'd struggled a lot this year after returning from Mexico. It wasn't just the actions on the trip, either; it was school. This last semester had been hard, and losing my friendship with Willow, Adalyn, and Hannah hadn't helped matters. I hadn't even been able to call my brother while he'd been away, so to have him home for a weekend meant a lot.

"Walker! Over here!" I shouted.

He glanced in my direction, waved, and made his way through the crowd to me.

"Hey, sis," he said, throwing his arms around me.

"Walker!" I cried, hugging him back. "It's so good to see you."

"You too. You look good. Thanks for coming to pick me up. I figured Mom would have wanted to be here as well," he said, looking around as if he were hoping she was going to jump out of some undisclosed location.

"Ah, yes, our mother. I offered to pick her up, but since Mr. Romance appeared, she's been... preoccupied."

"Ah, yes, Mr. Romance. Have you met him yet?" Walker asked as he held the door open for me.

I shook my head. "No, not yet. Not sure I really want to, given her track record. We'll just get used to him and he'll be gone, just like all the others."

"Can't say I blame you there... I feel the same way,

although she told me in her last email that this one was different," Walker replied, giving me a funny look.

I let out a laugh. "Oh yes, different. I think we have heard that before, haven't we?"

Walker nodded. "We have. I think it was guy two, five, and eight, or maybe it was five, seven, and twelve."

"No, I know it wasn't number eight. He was the one with that crazy laugh that she couldn't stand."

"No, that was seven. Number eight was the fire investigator that she met the night of the bar fire, remember?"

"Oh god, yes. How did I forget that? She was sure he was going to be the love of her life, and yet here we are, a new one again."

Walker laughed. "Do you know anything about him?"

I shook my head. "Not much. She's been unusually tight-lipped about him, but she did let it slip that this one comes with a new stepbrother. Apparently, he's about your age."

Walker looked at me with the same curious, annoyed look that I was sure had crossed my face the first time I'd heard about this man and had told Lorelai. It was just like Mom to drop this announcement on us. After all, she hadn't lost her freedom, and even though I'd always wanted to be like her, after the events of our girls' trip, I'd changed my mind. The shame from that night had been enough to stop me from dating since. I'd decided I was happy being boring old Aurora.

I popped the trunk on my car while Walker threw his duffel bag in, and then we climbed in. We were going to meet our new stepfather today. Apparently, Penelope had met him four months after I returned from Cozumel and had accepted his proposal a few weeks later. It was fast. She'd surprised me with a call only a couple of weeks ago and dropped the news that they had gotten married while on a trip to Vegas.

When I'd found out Walker would come home during my spring break, I made sure to be available to be here. It was the perfect opportunity for us to meet this man, and I was happy to not have to do it alone.

"So do you know much about the stepbrother?" Walker questioned.

I shook my head as I pulled off the highway. "Nothing really. Mom said he isn't around much. He travels a lot. Other than that, she has said nothing to me about him. I'd almost hedge a guess she's probably never met him herself, given the rush of the entire relationship."

"That figures." Walker shook his head.

"Can you check the address on that piece of paper in the middle console?"

Walker picked up the paper. "69 Fletcher Cresent."

"Okay. I was sure that was what it was." I said, turning into one of the wealthiest areas of Vancouver.

As we drove through the neighbourhood filled with houses as big as we'd ever seen, Walker let out a whistle.

"Looks like Mom finally did something right." He chuckled. "This neighbourhood is filled with a lot of doctors, lawyers, and I've heard the occasional sports stars."

I giggled. "Maybe it's her divorce lawyer from husband number four."

"Ha, that wouldn't be funny. That guy hated me." Walker chuckled.

"Well, you're different now. You've cleaned up your life."

We both looked at one another and laughed. I turned onto Fletcher Cresent, and within seconds we spotted number 69. I slowed my old beater of a car down and pulled into the driveway.

I'd just cut the engine when I saw Mom wave from the front door. Then she pushed it open and ran out into the driveway. She looked radiant in a white dress, especially with her dark tan.

"You ready?" Walker questioned.

"Not really, but there is no turning back now. She's already spotted us."

Walker chuckled and pushed his door open at the same time I did, and we both climbed out of the car and walked around to the front of it where we met Mother. She immediately threw her arms around both of us, pulling us in for a hug.

"Gosh, you two look great. I've missed you both so much," she said, now hugging us individually. "I'm so glad you are both here."

When she grabbed me, she pulled me against her. "Come on, come inside and meet Joe," she said, pulling us toward the door.

She hadn't even asked Walker how his first nine months had been. She hadn't asked me how school was going, if I was passing or failing, or worse, had dropped out. It shouldn't have surprised me. It was just like her; nothing had changed. She was and always would be solely focused on herself.

We stepped inside the house. I slipped my shoes off and then followed Walker, who followed Mom. I could tell he was just as uncomfortable in this house as I was. As Mom entered the kitchen, Walker glanced over his shoulder at me.

"Are you as stumped as I am?" he whispered.

I gave him a crooked smile. "Sure am. This is effed-up," I said through clenched teeth.

We stepped into the kitchen. "Aurora, Walker, this is Joe," Mom said, introducing him as Walker came to stand beside me. He was a very attractive, well-built older man, and it surprised me to see him at the counter making a tray of drinks. It was usually my mother doing those things.

"Walker," he said, shaking my brother's hand, "nice to meet you."

Then he turned to me. "Aurora, nice to meet you as well. Your mother has told me lots about both of you, and I look forward to getting to know each of you better. I also look forward to being your stepfather," he said, coming over and hugging me.

He smiled at me and then went back over to finish making the drinks while Mom started going on about how proud she was of both of us. We looked at one another as we listened to her go on like she was the one responsible for our schooling and career decisions, when the truth was, if you asked her, she'd barely even know what I was in school for.

"My dear, how about the four of us retire out back by the pool?" Joe said. "Dylan will be here shortly, I'm sure. Then I'll get some food on the barbeque. I know he's looking forward to meeting you both," Joe said, putting his hand on Mom's lower back and guiding her toward the back door.

Mom grabbed the tray of drinks and carried them outside while we followed. The backyard was amazing. A huge in-ground pool sat in the centre of a very well landscaped backyard. Walker and I took a seat at the table and helped ourselves to a drink.

"Oh, I know the two of you are going to love Dylan. He's been looking forward to meeting you both as well," Mom said, giggling as Joe tapped her behind.

I glanced at my brother, who gave me a look of disbelief before taking a drink.

"We are looking forward to meeting him. What does he do?" Walker asked.

"Dylan is the centre for the Vancouver Dominators," Joe announced.

"Holy hell. Seriously?" Walker asked. "Now I'll know two of them."

I shook my head. It looked like Walker was going to be pulled to the dark side with our mother, leaving me to fend for myself in this nightmare. Lorelai's brother played for the Dominators as well, and since they were and had always been Walker's favourite team, I could only imagine how excited he was.

"Yep." Joe smiled. "Who else do you know?" he questioned.

I cleared my throat. "Phil Anderson is my best friend's brother. He plays for them as well."

"Ah, yes, he plays right defense. He's an excellent player," Joe said.

Instantly, my brother began asking him questions, and his eyes lit up at every answer. He was beaming by the time Joe invited him inside to show him some things, leaving me alone outside with Mom.

I stood there looking around the backyard, tension building between us. She'd been on me for the past few months about dating. I let out a sigh as I looked at the gardens, praying for Walker to return, when she cleared her throat.

"So, have you met anyone at school?" she asked, pouring me another drink.

I shook my head.

"You know, you really should take some time to get to know some guys in your classes."

"I'm just trying to focus on getting good grades, Penelope."

"I ran into Willow the other day. She asked how you were doing. She says you've been distant since Cozumel."

I rolled my eyes. It was just like my mother to try and pull information out of me. She'd never even asked me how that trip had gone. It didn't matter anyway because she was the last person I'd tell anything about that trip.

"Is that so? Did she say anything else?" I said, fishing to find out if she'd told my mother about my lack of judgment on that trip.

"Nothing," she answered, looking at me. "Did

something happen on that trip between the two of you that you'd like to talk about?"

I almost choked on the lemonade as those words fell from her mouth. I wasn't sure if it was the fact she asked or the fact that she actually thought I'd talk to her about it. Regardless, I grabbed a napkin, wiped the lemonade from my chin, and shook my head.

"No, Mom. All is fine. We're just on different paths. So why don't you tell me where you met Joe?"

I sat there listening to her every once in a while, zoning out as I thought about my friends. Since we'd returned, I'd only kept in touch with Lorelai, but then we were the only ones who were finishing up our classes at the University of Victoria. The others had gone to the University of Toronto, but I'd heard through the grapevine Willow had dropped out of her program because of family issues and had returned to Vancouver.

"So that is why you are here," my mother said loud enough to pull me away from my thoughts.

I hadn't heard a word she said, but judging from her smile, I was sure I'd find out without having to ask again.

"I see."

The sliding door to the patio opened and out walked Joe and Walker, both talking up a storm. Mom smiled while I shifted in my seat. Walker looked like he was walking on cloud nine.

"God, I can't believe I'm actually going to meet him," he said, clapping his hands together. "Thanks for showing me all that stuff. What a rush," Walker said, coming and sitting down beside me.

"He should be here any minute," Joe said, glancing at his watch.

"Excuse me, but I need to use the washroom," I said, standing up.

"Sure thing. Just make a left down the hall from the kitchen door. It's the first door on your right." Joe smiled, opening the door for me.

I PULLED my phone from my pocket once I had locked the door to the bathroom and quickly texted Lorelai. I'd told her I'd let her know what was up the moment I found out.

Aurora: So, Penelope's big surprise... she's married to a man whose son is a Dominator

Lorelai: WHAT???? Aurora, what are you talking about?

Aurora: My mother married a man who's the father to one of the Vancouver Dominators

Lorelai: Oh god. Your brother must be beside himself. Have you met him yet? Who is it? I'll have to tell Phil.

Aurora: Nope, have not met him yet. He is apparently on his way over.

Lorelai: What's your new surprise stepfather like?

Aurora: Little different from the others. He lives over in the ritzy part of Vancouver. My car looks like a sore thumb in the driveway. Oh, and he actually wears full shirts, not wife beaters. Penelope has officially stepped up. He made drinks for everyone instead of standing over Penelope and demanding she do it. It's like an alternate reality.

Lorelai: Sounds like a complete 360.

Aurora: You think? Something has got to be wrong with the entire picture.

Lorelai: Maybe she has changed.

> Aurora: Do you remember Penelope?
> LOL

> Lorelai: Your mom, despite her faults, all of her faults, deserves to be with a decent guy, you know.

I TAPPED the side of my phone as I recounted the steps of the events so far tonight. I hadn't been able to remember anything being out of place in this picture, except for my mother.

> Aurora: I'm sure the whole thing will blow up once this guy doesn't treat my mother like trash.

> Lorelai: Maybe she is looking for a change.

I HEARD some footsteps in the hallway and a murmur of voices. I bet my new stepbrother was here.

Aurora: Got to go. I think the stepbrother is here. I'm hiding in the bathroom, and before they get suspicious, I need to make an appearance.

Lorelai: Text me later. I want to know who it is, and I want to hear all about the evening. I don't think I can wait until you get home.

Aurora: Okay, I'll let you know the instant I find out. Then you can ask your brother about him and let me know if he is a decent guy.

Lorelai: Will do. Have fun.

I POCKETED MY PHONE, flushed the toilet, and opened the door a crack to see the hallway empty. I shut the light off and made my way into the kitchen where I could see my mother standing beside Joe and Walker, talking with someone I couldn't see. Certain that must be him, I grabbed my drink from the counter where I left it and opened the back door.

They were chatting away when my mother finally noticed me.

"Ah, and Dylan, this is my daughter, Aurora."

I looked up just as Joe stepped to the side and caught sight of a pair of blue eyes I'd have known anywhere. Heat filled my body, and everything fell away until I heard the glass I'd been holding shatter as it hit the stone of the deck.

"Oh, my god. I'm so sorry," I said as the realization of what happened hit me.

My mother ran into the kitchen to get the broom, while Joe assured me that accidents happen. Walker and he bent down to pick up the large pieces of glass, while I stood there, my eyes locked with Dylan's.

I'd barely heard a word any of them said because I couldn't tear my eyes away from the guy standing in front of me. How on earth was it even possible that the man I'd had a one-night stand with would end up being my stepbrother? This seemed like a cruel joke the universe had played on my one and only spontaneous moment. Dylan didn't miss a beat though and acted like we'd never seen one another before.

"Aurora," he said, bringing his hand out for me to shake.

I could see nothing but laughter in his eyes as I slowly brought my hand to his and swallowed hard. The second our hands touched, my body heated, and the room spun.

"Aurora, you don't look very good," I heard my

mother say as she reached out and grabbed my shoulders. "Are you feeling alright?"

"I, uh, I don't feel so good," I mumbled. My mouth had gone dry, and I could barely swallow.

"Come inside with me," she immediately said, pulling me away from the situation. Once inside the kitchen, she had me sit down. She grabbed a cloth and wet it, placing it on the back of my neck. Then she poured me a glass of juice, placed it in front of me, then leaned on the counter in front of me, looking me directly in the eyes.

"What is going on?" she questioned, studying my face. "You look like you've seen a ghost. I know he is famous and all, but please."

"It's not that," I mumbled, taking a drink of my juice.

"Well then, what on earth is it? You don't act like this when you meet someone new. So spill it."

I drank the rest of my juice and looked at my mother. I wondered if this whole new situation she found herself in would make her act more like a mother. I needed to tell someone what had happened. I let out the breath I was holding.

"Could we go somewhere a little more private?"

My mother shook her head, let out a breath, and smiled. "Of course."

She led me down the same hall I'd gone down to

the washroom, and we stepped into a large office. She shut the door and turned, crossing her arms over her chest.

"What is it?" she questioned.

"Mexico."

"What about Mexico?"

I paced back and forth, my stomach actually spinning as I tried to form the words that I wanted to say.

"Alright, don't get angry."

"Aurora, please just tell me what is going on."

"I had a one-night stand in Mexico with a guy. I never got his name."

"Okay, I don't understand what that has to do with tonight, though. Is it something you just felt you needed to tell me, because you could have told me when you got back. You didn't need to wait until tonight, nine months later" she said as she went to pull open the door.

I closed my eyes. I could feel my heart beating hard in my chest, and I was getting dizzy again. My stomach turned as I tried to muster up the words. Penelope stepped out into the hall, and I knew I had to stop her from going back out there. "It was Dylan," I said loud enough she could hear.

I could feel the tears building, and I knew my face was probably as red as a tomato, but I mustered up the courage to look my mother in the eyes. She was quiet for a moment, studying me, and just when I thought she was going to come and comfort me, she burst into laughter.

Horrified, I wiped my eyes and glared at my mother.

"What is so funny?"

"Oh god, this is too much," she said, still laughing.

"Mom, it's not funny," I said, horrified.

She wiped at the tears that were rolling down her cheeks. "Oh, Aurora, lighten up. It's not that big of a deal. So what? So, you two bumped uglies. Do you realize I'd actually slept with my divorce lawyer before my last divorce? We'd met one night at a bar, and he'd taken me back to his place. Eighteen months later, I walked into his office to hire him to get me out of the mess I was in."

"Mom! This isn't about you and some lawyer," I cried.

"Aurora, how many times do I need to tell you? Life is about experiences! I bet he was a great experience for you."

I literally wanted to die. This was exactly like her. Why I thought she'd care was beyond me, and I'd been right. She didn't give a shit.

"Mom, this is embarrassing."

"Oh, Aurora, how many times do I have to tell you,

life is to be lived, to take chances, to have fun? That was what you were doing. Nothing wrong with it."

She wrapped her arms around me and pulled me into her.

"Mom, can't you see I'm a mess?" I questioned.

"I can, and you know what I say is an excellent remedy for that. Drinks. So, let's go get some and join the guys out back."

She rubbed my shoulder before opening the door and laughed again as she glanced back at me. "My uptight little bird finally spread her wings," she muttered.

I followed her back into the kitchen, where she poured each of us another drink, adding an extra shot of gin to mine. I made eye contact with her as she screwed the cap back onto the bottle. Why I'd ever wanted to be like her, I'd never know.

"Come on now. Time to act like nothing has happened."

I let out the breath I was holding as my stomach continued to turn. "What if I can't?"

"You can! Although, you will never know what might happen later on." She winked as she made her way to the patio door and slid it open.

"Is everything alright?" I heard Joe ask as we stepped out onto the patio.

"Oh, heavens yes. I'm sorry about that. Aurora and her issues," she said, giggling as she stepped outside.

I was ready to kill Penelope. I held my breath as I stepped out onto the back deck. My brother and Dylan sat talking. Immediately, Dylan looked over at me while Walker continued talking. I was going to go over and sit beside my mother when Dylan grabbed the chair beside him and pulled it toward him, slapping the seat.

"Come on over here and sit with us." He grinned.

If I were going to get through this night, there was one thing I was going to need, and that was a lot more gin.

Chapter 5

Dylan

Aurora had barely touched any of the food that my father made. She'd picked at her salad, barely touched the steak, and sat there looking like she was still about to throw up. To be honest, I was in shock that she was here in my father's house, but I was happy to see her.

Over the past nine months, I'd kicked myself almost daily for not getting the name or number of the girl I'd met in Cozumel. I'd relived the night over and over in my mind. When I'd woken the next morning to an empty bed, I realized how stupid I'd been. Now fate had stepped in and handed her to me on a silver platter. Or perhaps it was gold. Whatever it was, I was glad to see her again. I just wished she looked the same. Instead, she avoided my eyes and looked like she was going to be sick.

"Don't like steak?" I questioned as I leaned in close enough to her to catch a whiff of her. She wore the same coconut scented body lotion that she had on that night, a scent I hadn't been able to forget.

"I'm surprised she hasn't inhaled it." Walker chuckled. "Aurora loves meat."

She looked at me and I winked, then grabbed the pitcher from the centre of the table. "Anyone for more drinks?" I asked.

"Oh, yes, please," Penelope said, while grabbing Joe's glass as well.

I poured everyone a glass and added a little more to my own, then looked at Aurora and poured more into hers. She needed to relax a little.

"Well, she doesn't like to eat, but she sure loves to drink." I chuckled, watching as she reached for the glass. I'd watched her down at least four of my father's killer cocktails without food. I'd only guess she'd been feeling something by now.

"So, when do you play again?" Penelope asked.

"Thursday."

"Will you be able to attend the party on Saturday?"

I nodded and glanced over to see Aurora tear her eyes away from me.

"Aurora, you'll be here for the party, won't you?" I questioned, hoping she'd bring those pretty green eyes to mine.

"Of course she will be, along with Walker," Penelope answered.

"Oh, Mom, I'm not sure about that. I had to get special clearance to come here tonight. Not sure if my commander will allow it," Walker answered.

"So you have to get special clearance every time you want to attend something?" I questioned.

"Pretty much every time I leave the base. Especially while I'm in training."

"Wow, that is crazy. Well, hopefully we will see you," Joe added.

"Aurora, want to help me with the dishes?" Penelope questioned.

Aurora only nodded and began collecting dishes.

"Boys, let's retire to the family room, shall we? Dylan, you can show Walker some of your hockey videos while the girls clean up," Joe announced.

"Come on. I may even have a jersey here that I can sign for you," I said, getting up and slapping Walker on the shoulder.

"Oh man, I'd love that."

THE CONVERSATION TURNED AWAY from hockey once Penelope and Aurora joined us in the den.

"You know, I think we should show the kids around. What do you think?" Joe asked Penelope. "Show them where they will stay if they come here."

"I think we should," she agreed, getting up and joining Joe.

"Come on, Dylan, why don't you do the honours?"

I glanced over at Aurora, who was now leaning up against the bookcases, playing with her phone. She'd barely looked at me since she'd come back in here. She finally looked up and over at her mother.

"Mom, I'm going to skip the tour. I need to take care of something for school. Lorelai is messaging me. She needs help with something," she said, meeting my eyes briefly.

"Oh okay. No problem. I can show you around after." Penelope laughed.

"Come on, Dylan," Joe said.

"You know, I think I'm going to check in with the team. See how the interviews went," I muttered, pulling my phone from my pocket. Immediately, I noticed Aurora squinting in my direction. That had caught her attention.

"Alright, well, that leaves the three of us." Penelope giggled, taking hold of Walker's arm and pulling him out of the room.

I sat down on the couch, pretending to text, glancing over at Aurora occasionally. The second she lifted her eyes and looked my way, I smiled, but she quickly averted her eyes and stood up, turning her back to me.

I was finished playing this game. I got up from where I was sitting. She stood in the back of the room, facing the bookshelves, and I knew everyone else was far enough away that they were clearly out of earshot. With her face in her phone, she hadn't noticed I had moved to her side of the room. I placed both hands against the shelves and boxed her in.

"You're still thinking about that night, aren't you?" I whispered, my lips practically grazing her ear, the sweet smell of coconut filling my nose.

She stood still, her chest rising and falling in rapid succession.

"I bet you still get wet thinking about that night. I know I get hard as a fucking rock thinking about you," I whispered, this time my lips touching the shell of her ear.

Her body stiffened, and she spun around and lifted

her head enough that she could meet my eyes and shook her head while swallowing hard. I could see her pulse beating on the side of her neck and her cheeks and chest were now flushed.

"It's enough."

Her voice, while a little forceful, shook as she spoke. I thought it was cute how she was trying to control everything in this moment, when in fact her body and eyes were betraying her. I could already see the want, the need, in them.

"That's too bad," I whispered, bringing my hand to her cheek. "I've been dying to do this again." I brought my lips to hers.

She didn't fight me, so I deepened the kiss. She brought her fingers to the back of my head and let out a tiny whimper as she ran her fingers through my hair, which was when I pulled my lips from hers and my hand from her cheek. She stood there, her eyes closed, rocking back and forth a little. When she opened her eyes, the look she gave me gave her away. She still wanted me.

"Dylan, we can't do this. That night was…"

"Magical. I know." I winked.

"A one-time thing," she corrected.

"Is that so?"

She shook her head and licked her lips. My eyes fell to her chest. She was still breathing hard, and I could see the outline of her perfect nipples through that sweater. Nipples I'd love to suck on again.

"So, are you telling me you don't want another shot with me?" I asked, bringing my hands up and grazing her breasts ever so slightly.

The instant my hands connected with her breasts, she closed her eyes and let out a tiny moan.

She nodded but said nothing.

"That isn't want your body is saying," I whispered.

"I...I...it can't happen again," she said, placing her hands on my chest.

I couldn't help but smirk. "Is that so?"

She nodded, bringing her hands down from my chest. She turned away from me. It was then I wrapped my arm around her waist and brought her body back against mine.

With my free hand, I brushed her hair away from her neck and brought my lips to her soft skin, sucking hard enough I knew I'd leave a mark. I felt her body weaken in my arms as I kissed her neck. I continued small kisses and finally tipped her head back a bit and brought my lips to hers, my tongue parting hers. I swiped through her mouth. She didn't pull away; she didn't fight me. Instead, her body melted against mine, and like before, she kissed me back.

I allowed my hands to wander a little, bringing one up over her breast. I figured that would be a telltale sign. If she didn't want this, she'd freak the hell out. Instead of fighting me, she arched her back, pressing her breast into my hand as her lips moved over mine.

I broke our kiss and looked into her eyes. She stood against me, breathing hard. "Just imagine how explosive it will be next time," I muttered as I heard voices approaching. "The next time I fuck that sweet pussy." I ran my hand down her flat stomach and between her legs, then made my way back to the other side of the room where I'd been sitting before and acted as if nothing had happened. She stood there, her mouth open, staring in my direction as Penelope, Walker, and my father entered the room, all of them laughing.

I looked across the room as they all sat down to see Aurora still staring my way. The look in her eyes said it all. She wanted me as much as I wanted her, and I'd be damned if I gave up that easily.

"WANT to go grab some breakfast? I'm starved," Knox asked, climbing into the driver's seat and starting the engine.

We always went to early-morning practices together. Knox normally dragged his ass, but this morning, I was dragging mine. I'd gotten home late last night and had tossed and turned at the fact I'd been so close to having her again.

"What the hell got into you today?" Knox asked, once he was in the car.

"What do you mean?"

"Well, first, you weren't anywhere near ready when I showed up and you played like shit."

"I did not."

"Fuck me, yes, you did. You seemed distracted."

"So what? Haven't you been distracted before?"

"I have…but…"

"But what? Are you the only one who's allowed to be distracted?" I grumbled.

Knox tapped the steering wheel as we came to a stoplight. He reached down and turned the radio down a little lower and glanced over at me.

"It's almost like we are repeating the few weeks after you returned from Mexico all over again."

I clenched my jaw and looked out the window. It was Mexico all over again, only this time it was worse. I hadn't known what to do when I saw her standing there in front of me. All I knew was that during those few seconds when I saw her again, I wanted her in a way I'd never felt before.

"Or maybe I'm thinking wrong. You were relaxed after Mexico, not so pissy. You're acting like you did when you found out about Carlie. Yeah, that is more like it," Knox said, pulling into the breakfast diner we always went to and parking the car. "She hasn't been bothering you again has she?"

Carlie had been a hellish nightmare for me. Not only had she broken my heart, dragged me through the mud, and tried to ruin my career, but she'd stalked me for the better part of five months and slandered me all over social media. I'd had a right to be pissy during that time, and anyone who said differently was an ass. It had ended with me being forced to send a cease-and-desist letter written by my own lawyers and the team's when I began losing contracts left, right, and centre.

"No, she's been non-existent, which I am hoping continues on."

"Then what has you so bothered?"

We entered the diner, sat down, and placed our usual order. Then Knox looked over at me, waiting impatiently.

I let out a sigh. "You were right the first time. Remember Mexico?" I questioned.

Knox nodded, turning his attention to me.

"Remember the girl."

"Yeah, the one you couldn't forget. The one you turned celibate for."

"I didn't turn celibate. I'm not the type to just jump in the sack with whatever moves, you know that."

Knox shook his head and chuckled. I was probably the only guy on the team that hadn't had a different woman in his bed each night while on the road. Well, aside from the married guys.

"What I know is that you are fucked up." Knox chuckled.

"Call me what you want. Anyway, back to the girl."

"Okay, what about her? If you are going to tell me you still wish you'd gotten her name, I think I might be sick."

That was just like Knox. He wasn't the type of guy who got into deeply committed relationships; he was more the hit it and quit it type. It was fine, it worked for him. I just wasn't built that way.

"No, I found out who she was."

"Oh, well, do tell."

The server dropped our mushroom omelets down in front of us and poured us both a little more coffee, smiled, and walked away. I watched as Knox added a generous amount of hot sauce to his omelet before passing the bottle over to me.

"Remember how I told you my father got remarried."

"Oh god, don't you dare tell me she's your new stepmother." Knox chuckled. "That would be fucking fantastic."

"Nope, stepsister."

"Get the fuck out of here," Knox said, lifting his head to look at me.

"Yep. She still wants me, I still want her, and I'm not going to stop until I get her."

"What's your father going to say about that?" Knox asked.

I thought for a moment. My father shouldn't have a single thing to say about anything. He wasn't perfect by any means, and his track record showed it. Besides, he had no right to tell me who I could and couldn't date, nor who I could and couldn't love.

"He never did like Carlie."

"Can't say I blame him there. She was a bitch, man."

"Not at first."

"Yes, at first. She was awful. I'd have cut her loose ages before you did. She was only after you for the money anyway. Perhaps your father saw that."

"I doubt it. My father liked no one I brought home. Besides, I'm not looking for his approval."

"Man, you know you are in trouble, right? I mean, what if she wants nothing to do with you?"

"She already tried that. I proved her wrong, and I'll continue proving her wrong until she admits she is wrong. She wants me, I can tell. She practically crumbled in my arms when I touched her."

"Okay, if you say so. I'm telling you, man, you are in trouble." Knox chuckled.

He didn't need to say anything else. I already knew I was in trouble. Far more trouble than I could even comprehend. Somehow though, I knew she was worth every second of it.

Chapter 6

Aurora

"What are you going to have?"

I glanced up from the menu and looked across the table at Lorelai. I'd been in a daze for days, and today was no different.

"What?"

"I asked what you were going to have?" Lorelai frowned. "Are you worried about something? Is Professor Johnson giving you trouble again?"

It was a good guess. I'd had trouble with Professor Johnson earlier on in the year, but things had sorted themselves out. I just shrugged and looked back at the menu in front of me, still not really reading the words, just staring off into space and thinking about the other night.

"Aurora?"

"Huh?" I said, looking up again.

Lorelai sat there, frowning at me, a hint of concern in her eyes. "What is going on, Aurora? You've been like this all week. Not making full notes. Actually, you've barely made any notes all at, and then you borrow mine at night. We've been sitting here for twenty-five minutes in your favourite restaurant, and you still haven't even decided what you want to eat yet, when normally you don't even need to look at the menu. So, what is going on?"

I glanced around the room, the familiarity of the restaurant coming to me. I'd basically zoned out the moment I'd gotten into the car to come from my mother's three days ago, because the only thing on my mind had been Dylan. I'd said nothing to Lorelai about that night, even though she'd asked me many times who my new stepbrother was. Instead, I'd suffered in silence, trying to figure out why my luck was so damn bad. The hottest, sexiest, most riveting night of my young life with a man, and it had to turn out this way.

"Earth to Aurora!" Lorelai shouted, snapping her fingers in front of my face.

I jumped and met my friend's eyes. "Sorry. I think I'll have the salmon."

"Great, now tell me what the hell is going on? Like I said, you've been like this for days."

I let out the breath I was holding and sank down into my chair. "My life is over," I muttered.

"What are you talking about?" Lorelai laughed.

"I don't know where I am going to apply for a job at the end of the year," I muttered.

"Okay?" Lorelai frowned. "Where is this coming from? We are at the top of our class, and I already told you Phil is going to get us in with the Dominators."

I sighed. "We can't work for the Dominators," I mumbled, fear filling me. We'd been planning to apply since we'd finished our first year in school. Lorelai's brother was going to go to bat for us, and he promised if we kept our grades up, it would almost be a sure thing. He'd come through, landing us both an interview in the next month or so.

Lorelai shook her head and crossed her arms in front of her chest just as the server returned to the table.

"Any ideas?" he questioned.

"She'll have the salmon, and I'll have the chicken," she said, not giving me a chance to change my mind. He nodded and left, going to put our order in.

"Okay, so tell me, why can't we work for the Dominators?"

"Because of Dylan."

In my mind, I was making perfect sense. To Lorelai, she did not know who Dylan even was, so she just sat there, her face contorted in confusion, waiting for me to explain.

"Who the hell is Dylan?" she asked.

"Remember the guy in Cozumel?" I asked.

Lorelai frowned. "The guy you slept with, the one-nighter, who, according to you, was the best sex you'd ever had? The guy and his friend who I thought looked familiar? That guy?"

"Yes, that guy," I said, picking up my pop and taking a drink.

"Are you having some kind of meltdown I should know about?" Lorelai questioned with concern. "You never got the guy's name, and I don't have a clue what he has to do with you acting this way or why we can't work with the Dominators."

"Can't you keep up?" I gritted.

Lorelai glanced around the room like she was looking for a hidden camera or something. Then she looked back at me. "Aurora, I can keep up, but you aren't making any sense. Why don't you just start from the beginning? Phil has worked hard to get us interviews with the head of their therapy division with the

Dominators. I'd hate for us not to show up and take the interview."

I gritted my teeth together. I did not know why she was making this so much more difficult on me than it had to be. Yet instead of getting angry, I took a deep breath and looked over at my friend.

"I know he has. Your brother is one of the best there is," I said, feeling kind of bad now that I wasn't sure that was the best course of action to take for work.

"I know. I also know we can't spit in his face that way. He's doing us a huge favor. He's gone out on a limb for us."

I let out a sigh. "Okay, so the guy in Cozumel."

"Yes."

"I never got his name, remember?"

"Correct, and you were kicking yourself in the ass for weeks after. Probably still are, which is probably why you are completely messed up, because you're missing some of that good old loving right now."

I played with my straw and nodded. "Correct."

"So???"

"I know who he is."

Lorelai almost dropped her glass. She placed it at the back of the table and looked over in my direction. "What? How?"

"His name is Dylan, and he's one of the Vancouver

Dominators!" I said, not really wanting to divulge how I even knew that.

"Oh my god, you've got to be kidding me. The best sex of your life plays on the team with my brother. I've told you that you need to watch hockey. It wouldn't have taken you so long to figure it out." Lorelai giggled.

"It's not funny, and I'm not joking."

"Okay, sorry," Lorelai said, rolling her eyes. "So, how did you find that out? Did you see him on TV? Did your brother take you to a game where you ran into him? Which, if he did, I'm going to be pissed you didn't tell me," Lorelai said, picking up her glass once again.

"He is my new stepbrother."

This time Lorelai's glass slipped from her hand and smashed on the floor. She stared at me and then looked down, embarrassment flooding her face as she realized she'd broken the glass.

"Wow. Now it's not a wonder why I thought he looked familiar."

"I bet Walker and him will get along well."

If she only knew. I shook my head, still not sure she believed me.

"Okay, tell me, this supposed hockey stepbrother… is his room covered in hockey posters and shit? Phil's was until Candace dug her claws into him. It's funny how suddenly they grow up." She giggled, her eyes lighting up as our food finally arrived.

The server had barely placed hers down before she was snatching fries off the plate.

"Sorry I broke the glass," she said, pointing to the floor.

"Not a problem. I'll get that cleaned up and grab you both another refill." He winked and took off in the direction in which he'd come.

"It's not the way you envision it completely," I muttered, swirling my fork around in the bed of pasta beneath the salmon.

"What isn't?"

"The whole situation."

"Okay????" She smiled. "Why don't you tell me this little dream of yours?" She giggled again, shaking her head.

"You don't believe me," I said, looking over at my friend, who sat there smiling.

Lorelai laughed. "I'm sorry, Aurora, this story is a little much, especially for you. If it were coming from say Willow, I'd believe it."

"I'm not joking, Lorelai. My stepbrother is the Dominator, and he is the guy I spent the night with in Cozumel." I sighed, feeling one weight rise off my chest, only for another to press down. I knew she still wouldn't believe me, so I pulled the neck of my sweater down to show her the light purple mark that was still on my neck. The mark he'd left the other night.

Lorelai almost dropped her fork, but her quick reflexes allowed her to grab it before it hit the floor. Lorelai studied me for a moment. "You've got to be shitting me?"

"Seriously, I almost died when I saw him."

Lorelai sat there, still not knowing what to say. She studied me, then reached over and pulled my sweater down again and wiped her finger over the mark to make sure it didn't come off.

"Wow, Aurora, I don't really know what to say."

"Join the club." I sighed.

"What did he do? Did he recognize you? Never mind, that was a stupid question."

I nodded, placing a piece of salmon in my mouth. "Sure was."

"What was his reaction?"

I sat there, replaying the entire night over in my mind. Most people would have been mortified, but not Dylan.

"You don't want to know," I muttered.

"The hell I don't."

I couldn't help but laugh. Even though she was my best friend, I was hesitant to tell her everything. I didn't want her to think badly of me.

"He was all over me."

Lorelai lifted her eyes and met mine. "Are you serious? In front of everyone?"

I shook my head. "Only when we were alone, but he made it obvious that he knew me in front of everyone, or at least I think he did."

She almost jumped across the table at me. "What?"

"Yep, he wants to, um…continue things."

"What did you say?"

Just then the server approached the table with our refills and was about to ask if we needed anything else, but Lorelai beat him to it by shoving her hand out toward him and immediately telling him we were fine.

"What did you say?"

"What I should have said. No."

"Okay and…"

"What do you think? He wouldn't take that as an answer. So, instead, the second we were alone, he was all over me. Flirting, putting his hands on me, his lips on me, pulling me into him. He even said if I thought the first time was good, I couldn't imagine what it would be like the next time now that he knows my body."

I could feel my face heating at the memory of that night. At his words.

"Ohhhh my god.!!!!!" Lorelai screeched.

"Shut up!" I said, holding my hands out to a now excited Lorelai.

"I will not. You've got to think about this," she said.

"I don't, because there is nothing to think about."

Just then, my cell phone rang, and I looked down at the screen to see Walker's name appear.

"Is that him?" she asked, excitement growing in her voice.

"No. It's Walker. He'll be worried if I don't answer it."

"Fine, go ahead."

In a matter of minutes, I'd found out that Walker wouldn't be attending the wedding party on Saturday, which made me sad, but made me worry. I swallowed hard as I listened to him talk about the fact that his commanding officer wouldn't allow him leave. He sounded disappointed but nowhere near as disappointed as I would be on Saturday night. I'd be alone with Dylan in a house full of people.

I hung up the phone and looked over at Lorelai jumping right back to the beginning of the conversation.

"Bottom line, there is no way I can accept a job with the Dominators."

"If you think I'm turning down that interview my brother has worked so hard to get for us, you are mistaken. I'm also not turning down a job if I am lucky enough to be offered one. Now what did Walker want?"

I dragged my fork over my salmon and then took another bite, while I quickly figured out a solution for Saturday night. I was already being forced to go to the wedding party. There was no out for me. Then I glanced over at Lorelai who sat there eating her fries while looking around the restaurant. She hadn't seen my mom in a while, and I knew she'd be thrilled to see her.

"What are you doing Saturday night?"

She shrugged. "Probably working on my paper as should you be."

I nodded. "Feel like going to a wedding celebration party instead?" I questioned.

"I'll have to think about it." She shrugged. "I'm behind on my paper."

I shook my head. "Look, I'll do the interview, and I'll help you with your paper if you do this for me," I muttered.

Lorelai looked over at me, a hint of a smile on her lips. "Where is the party?"

Chapter 7

Dylan

I stepped through the front door and glanced at a group of unfamiliar faces. I probably should have brought Knox as my wingman for tonight, I thought to myself. These types of parties just weren't my style. In fact, no party was. I preferred being with my boys over being in a room full of people I didn't know.

I made my way to the kitchen and out onto the back deck, where I saw my father and Penelope talking with another couple. I lifted my hand and waved, letting them know I'd arrived. Then I made my way back inside.

I was still reeling from today's meeting with the coach about the entire team's performance at the last few games. He'd told us we had better get our shit together if we planned to make it to the playoffs this year. If we didn't, it would be the first year in five that we didn't make it. The entire tone of the meeting had put me in a mood that I'd been trying to shake off all day.

I made my way through the crowd of people, amazed that no one had stopped me yet. Usually, once they saw me, I was trapped. Tonight, I was on a mission, and even though I knew most of my father's friends would be eager to talk to me, that would have to wait.

I felt my phone vibrate. Pulling it from my pocket, I glanced at the screen to see Knox had messaged. They were going to Illusion and wanted to know if I wanted to go.

Dylan: Can't right now. Family obligation.

Knox: You aren't any fun.

Dylan: I know.

Knox: Maybe afterward?

Dylan: I'll message you to see if you are still there.

Knox: We will be. Clark and Harris want to blow off steam, maybe pick up a couple of chicks. You could probably use a release too.

I CHUCKLED TO MYSELF. He did not know how much of a release I needed, but I'd already set my sights on the prize I wanted.

Knox: So what do you say? In or out later?

Dylan: I'll message soon. I could blow off steam myself. As for picking up a chick, not my style man, I'm already working on a minor project.

I SHOVED my phone back into my pocket in time to see one of my father's friends making his way toward me. He always asked me a million questions, and I was looking for any way out of the conversation when out of the corner of my eye I caught sight of Aurora. She looked perfect. Her hair hung loose down her back. She was with another girl who was saying something to her, and she turned and smiled. The smile lit up the entire room. Then she stepped into the den and out of my sight.

"Dylan, good to see you. How's it going?"

"Good, Dixon, thanks for asking."

"Listen, I want to ask you what you think your chances are of hitting the playoffs this year? I've been watching, and I'll say I think it's a long shot."

"I'm happy to talk to you about this in a bit, but right now, I need to make an important call. Can I catch up with you soon?"

"Ah, yes, sure thing," Dixon added. "I know you're a busy man."

I shook his hand and made my way into the den. The room was full, and I searched the crowd, finally spotting her. She stood across the room talking up a storm with the other girl she was with. She hadn't spotted me yet, so I just took a seat on the couch and watched her.

My eyes skimmed her body. She looked amazing in the tight black tank top and white skirt she wore. I'd been waiting all week just to see her again, and I couldn't wait to talk to her. She laughed at something the other girl said, and then she nodded as the girl whispered something in her ear. The other girl walked away, leaving her standing there, alone, holding her glass in one hand as she glanced around at the other people in the room, finally spotting me. Almost immediately her face fell.

Once the room emptied a bit, I got up from where I was sitting and made my way over to her. She rolled her eyes and looked away, fidgeting with the glass she held. I couldn't help but smile at the light-pink hue that was rising to her cheeks and chest at my approach.

"Hey there," I said, coming up beside her. "Where did your bodyguard go?"

She let out a huff. "She isn't my bodyguard."

"Could have fooled me. She hasn't been away from you once tonight until now."

"What are you doing? Stalking me?"

"Like most girls, you wish I was stalking you." I chuckled.

Aurora shook her head and looked around the room. "What does it matter to you where she went?" she asked, locking her eyes with mine.

My eyes fell to her full lips, and all I wanted to do was bend down and take her mouth. I wanted to hear her moan again; I wanted to watch as her eyes looked up at me while I was buried inside of her.

She looked at me, but neither of us said anything.

"Why are you looking at me like that?" she questioned.

"Like what?"

"Like you could eat me?"

I chuckled. "Because I could. Actually, wait, I have." I winked.

Her cheeks flamed red, a frown settling on her face.

"Dylan, you can't talk to me that way."

"Actually, I can. If these people weren't surrounding us, I'd do more to you than just talk to you that way."

"You're impossible."

She was damn cute when she got flustered.

"No, I'm not. I'm speaking nothing but the truth."

She glared at me. "Just let it go already. I told you, it was a one-time thing."

"A one-time thing you are praying repeats itself." I winked and dropped my hand so my fingers could rub against the side of her thigh.

"I will not tell you again. Don't," she gritted.

It was as if she'd thrown down a challenge, and there was no way I was backing down. She didn't know who she was playing with.

"Or what?" I asked, leaning into her.

She turned away and left the room. I quickly followed behind. I mean, she must want me to follow her, right? She made her way toward the kitchen and then turned down the hall. I figured she was going to duck into the washroom, but she continued down the hall and made her way into the room at the end, so I followed.

I was just about to the door when she slammed it closed. I gave it a second and then opened it, stepping inside.

"Get out of here," she gritted.

"No. My house, remember?"

"God, you are so full of yourself."

I approached her, her eyes following my every move. "You don't mean that," I said.

"I do. I also meant it when I said what happened between us in Mexico was a one-time thing."

As I continued making my way toward her, she stepped back until she was up against the wall. I placed a hand on each side of her body. I could hear the shakiness in her breathing as she looked up at me.

"You can try to fool yourself into believing it was only a one-time thing, but we both know the truth. The response out of you when I kissed you last weekend was the same response I got down there. So stop trying to kid yourself," I whispered as I stared into her eyes. "You want it again. You want me again."

She locked eyes with mine, and she swallowed hard as she stared at me.

"You weren't that good," she said, her voice shaking and cracking.

"I beg to differ." I moved close enough my nose touched her cheek.

She smelled divine. Again, she wore the same coconut body lotion she'd used in Cozumel. The sweet scent flooded my nose. I could feel the warmth of her body, and the closer I got, the quicker her breathing picked up.

"You weren't. I barely even…"

It was then she closed her eyes and swallowed hard. When she opened them, she met mine. Her pupils were dilated, and her chest was now rising and falling faster.

"Are you going to tell me you barely came?" I whispered, my lips grazing her ear.

I looked into her eyes and allowed mine to wander. I could see the outline of her perfect nipples through her dress and almost immediately wanted to bring my mouth to them.

She slowly shook her head. "It's the truth," she said, breathing hard.

"Is it?"

She nodded, this time not saying anything.

"Tell you what. If you are telling me the truth right now, then you're probably not wet. Would that be correct?"

Her eyes widened at my question and her breathing picked up the pace as she looked at me.

"Tell me? Would I be right?"

She nodded.

I brought my hand to my chin and ran my fingers over my jaw. "Okay then. So if I were to reach into your panties, I'd find you drier than the Sahara? Correct?"

She nodded, her cheeks flushed, her chest rising and falling in rapid succession.

I dropped my hand from my jaw to the bottom of her short skirt and danced my fingers slowly along her inner thigh, making my way toward her centre.

I watched her. She closed her eyes, her breathing now quicker than before. "What…what are you doing?" she murmured, her voice shaking as her eyes fell to my lips.

I slipped her panties to the side and ran my fingers through her soaked center, closing my eyes as I felt her.

"Liar," I growled.

Almost immediately, her lips were on mine. Her arms wrapped around my neck as I kept her up against the wall and slid two fingers deep inside of her.

As my tongue parted her lips and washed through her mouth, she let out a tiny moan. I could feel myself straining against my jeans and had never been so happy when she lowered her hands and pulled at my belt, loosening it enough to open the button and drop the zipper.

"I hate you," she breathed heavily between kisses as she dug her hand into my pants and grabbed my hard cock.

"No, you don't," I whispered.

I pulled at the top of her dress, lowering it so I could have access to her amazing tits. The second they were bare, I brought my mouth to one of her perfect pink nipples and swirled my tongue around it, then sucked it into my mouth. She let out a moan loud enough that someone could have heard if it hadn't been for the music pumping through the house.

"No, I do," she said, breathing hard.

"That's fine. Then I hate you too," I replied as I moved my mouth to the other nipple.

I guided her away from the wall and over to the bed where I bent her over. I lifted her dress and pushed her panties to the side. Running my cock through her wetness, I reached into the drawer of the nightstand and grabbed a condom, ripped it open, and slid it on me. I pushed into her as she let out another loud moan as I buried myself inside of her.

"You still not going to come?" I questioned through clenched teeth as I bent over her.

She fisted the blankets on the bed as I pounded into her.

"You still not turned on?"

"Oh god," she cried.

"Tell me it feels good," I demanded, knowing full well she was getting closer.

She hissed as she fisted the blankets.

I reached around and pinched her nipples as I drove myself deep into her. I could already feel her tightening around me.

"Are you close?" I questioned, breathing hard.

She nodded as I continued to pinch and pull on her nipples.

"Say it."

"I'm close," she cried as she breathed hard.

"Do you want to come?" I questioned, slowing my pace.

"Yes."

"Should I rub your clit?" I asked.

"Please," she moaned, almost begging me.

Placing one hand on her shoulder, I pulled her back against me, forcing myself even deeper inside of her. I reached around and began stroking her clit, enjoying the feeling of her tightening around me. She began moaning and finally lowered her hand and placed it on top of mine, moving hers in pace with me.

I could feel the base of my spine tightening, but there was not a chance in hell I was going to come before she did. I picked up my pace, rubbing her clit faster as I continued pumping into her.

In seconds, I felt her tighten around me and a flood of wetness as she finally buried her face into the mattress and screamed as her orgasm flooded her body. The second that happened, I too felt my release. I placed my hand on the bed and braced myself as my orgasm ripped through my body.

In those seconds, everything fell away. I'd forgotten that the only thing separating us from a house full of people was the door to my old bedroom.

I pulled myself from her, grabbed a tissue from the box, and quickly removed the condom and placed it into the wastepaper basket. I turned away from her and took a quick second to adjust myself and do up my pants and belt. When I turned around, she'd already fixed her dress and stood there, looking at me.

I didn't give her a second to say anything. "What's your number?"

"Why?"

"Just give me your number," I said, opening up a contact card and turning the phone toward her so she could put her number in. "Don't think of giving me the wrong number, either. I don't want to call and ask your mother for it, or worse, your brother."

She looked up at me, rolled her eyes, and quickly hit the delete button, starting over again.

Once she handed my phone back to me, I quickly opened a message and sent her a text. The moment I saw her screen light up with my number, I knew it had gone through.

"Why did you do that?"

I chuckled before bringing my hand to her cheek and sliding it into her hair, bringing her lips to mine.

"Because after that…you are going to want to call me. It will torture you to wait, just like it's tortured me for nine months after our first time together."

Aurora looked at me, her cheeks still pink, her chest still rising and falling in rapid succession. "No, I won't."

"Mmmm, I beg to differ. I say I'll hear from you before the week is out."

I didn't wait for her to fight me. I went over to the door, opened it, and stepped out into the hall and made my way over to a group of guys that I normally spoke with. It was only a matter of minutes before I saw Aurora come around the corner from the hallway. She glanced in my direction, looking like she was going to come over to me, but then she spotted the girl she'd been with earlier and pulled her off in the opposite direction. Now all I had to do was wait.

Chapter 8

Aurora

I made my way into Sip and Stir on my way home and grabbed a cinnamon scone and muffin. I sat down at an empty table and pulled out my notes from my last class.

I split the scone in half and took a bite and was about to open my notes and go over them when I caught sight of my brother. He pulled the door open, walked in, and went straight to the counter. After he'd placed his order, he glanced over his shoulder, surprise lining his face as he smiled. He thanked the girl and made his way over to me.

"This is a pleasant surprise. What are you doing here?" he said, sliding into the booth across from me."

"Shouldn't I ask you that? It's not normal for you to be out here on the island."

"No, it's not. I have a work meeting not too far from here in about thirty minutes. So, I thought I'd come over a little early, stop at a couple of places, and then grab a coffee before I went."

"A work meeting? Something going on?" I questioned.

He chuckled. "You know I can't tell you anything about it."

"I know." I sighed, letting out a yawn.

"Everything alright? You look a little more tired than usual."

I shrugged. "Everything is fine. I guess it's just been a long week."

I thought back to dinner the other night, when I'd first re-encountered Dylan. I didn't even need to try hard, and I could still feel the same tension in my body when I'd met Dylan that night at Mom and Joe's. I was sure everyone in the room had noticed it, even though I'd silently prayed for days that they hadn't.

"Anything bothering you?" Walker questioned, looking at me with concern.

I shook my head and took another bite of the cinnamon delight, hoping I wasn't giving anything away. Most of my life, Walker had read me like a book, so I didn't know why I wasn't just telling him the truth. "No, everything is great. Why do you ask?"

"I don't know. You seemed funny the other night at Joe's. Especially when Dylan arrived."

I could feel a surge of heat run through my body. He had noticed, and now I wanted to die.

"What do you mean?" I questioned, trying hard to act like everything was completely normal.

"You seemed, I don't know, weird. Almost like you knew him."

I leaned back in the booth and sighed. There was no use keeping it from him. That statement right there told me he had already figured it out. Besides, we never kept secrets from one another.

"Okay, fine. Don't freak out."

"Why would I freak out? So you knew the guy, probably from Lorelai, no doubt. I mean, you two normally hang out at her brother's house, so it wouldn't surprise me you'd met him there."

"No, I didn't meet him through Phil. I met Dylan when we were in Mexico. We didn't exchange names or anything. We just spent the night together on what I'd call an idiotic and irresponsible night on my behalf."

"You're shitting me?" Walked asked, looking up at me, his coffee halfway to his mouth.

I shook my head. "No, I went on a mission to be more like Mom. I wanted one night to get over Greg. It was dumb and stupid and something that never ever should have happened. Anyway, you can imagine my surprise when I saw him again."

"You mean to tell me you didn't recognize him?"

"Why would I? I don't watch hockey."

"No, but Lorelai does. Did she not recognize him?"

I shrugged. "She said he looked familiar, but she couldn't place him. Then she got a bad sunburn and basically was of no use to anyone for the rest of the trip. Anyway, you can imagine my shock when I saw him."

Walker chuckled. "You might be right. Perhaps you really have the worst luck of anyone you or I know. Look, I got to be going or I'll be late. Try not to stress over it. It's in the past."

Walker got up and dumped his cup in the garbage, waved, then laughed again and made his way out the door of the coffee shop, leaving me sitting there alone. He did not know how badly I wished he were right and that the events of that night were truly in the past.

I LAY ON MY BED, staring at my textbook. I'd come home, ate half my dinner, then came into my room. I needed to study, but I couldn't stop thinking of Dylan. In fact, I'd barely stopped thinking of him since he followed me into the bedroom on Saturday night.

"You'd better snap out of this mood you are in and get ready to have a good time tonight," Lorelai said, coming into my room and dropping her books on my desk. She sat down on my favourite reading chair and spun around to look at me. "Sophie and Mila will be here in a couple of hours."

I dropped my pencil and rested my head on my arm. "What if I don't want to go out tonight?"

"It's Friday, why wouldn't you want to go out tonight?" Lorelai asked, giving me a funny look.

I let out a sigh and tried to come up with any reason that made sense, but I couldn't think of anything. The only thing I could come up with was because I wanted to stay home and drool over someone I was trying not to want.

"See, you really want to go out tonight," she said, getting up and making her way over to my closet. She opened the door and began skimming through my clothes, trying to find something to wear.

"No, I really don't." I pouted.

Lorelai stopped what she was doing and made her

way over to where I lay on my bed. She plopped down beside me and studied me. "What is it?"

I rolled over and stared up at the ceiling, not sure what to tell my best friend. I'd kept the events of the Saturday-night bedroom encounter all to myself.

"If something is bothering you, you know you can tell me." she said, waiting for me to break down and share with her. "You have been weird since the party, so I'm going to guess something happened between the time I went to the washroom and then helped your mom in the kitchen. Didn't it?"

Lorelai was like a mind reader. It was something I found so fascinating about her. She could always tell when someone was having trouble. She always said she was more in tune with other people than with herself, and that was why she always got hurt so badly.

I nodded. "You're right."

"Well, why don't you tell me what happened? Maybe I can help you sort through the issue."

I literally wanted to die. I was so ridiculously attracted to Dylan that I did not know how to navigate the things I was feeling. He was my new stepbrother. There shouldn't be any type of attraction to him now that our families had joined. He should have been just as annoying to me as Walker could be. Instead, every time he looked my way or was near me, my heart instantly sped up and I got a funny feeling in the pit of my stomach. His actions on Saturday night had blown my mind, and I hated my body for responding the way it had.

"You like him, don't you?" she questioned.

I ran my hand over my face and nodded. "Yes."

"Then why are fighting it so hard? I mean, it's not like you are cousins or something."

I shrugged. "What will people think?"

"People don't have to know," Lorelai whispered.

"I know, but I know."

Lorelai let out a sigh. "Okay, but you told your mother what happened in Mexico. She wasn't upset."

"No, on the contrary, she found it rather hilarious," I said, looking at my best friend. "I'm not sure why I had expected anything less."

"Then what is the issue?"

"We slept together the other night," I blurted out.

"When?" She frowned. "You've been here all week."

The second I looked at her, her mouth dropped open in shock. "At the party????"

I nodded.

"With all those people?"

Again, I nodded. "Then he gave me his number and is expecting me to message him. In fact, it was almost like he challenged me."

"Why didn't you message him?"

"Have you ever known me to do anything when I'm challenged to do it?"

Lorelai smirked. "Oh boy. He really likes you too, then."

"Yeah. I mean, I think he does."

"I say just get with him, or tonight, maybe pick up a guy. Whatever you do, you need to get him out of your system. There is only one of two ways to do that. Either you succumb to your desire and go for him, or you go for someone else."

For the first time I could remember, Lorelai was actually zero help to me. I'd no idea what the answer was, but since Saturday, I couldn't remember how many times I'd picked up my cell phone to message him, stopping myself each time. It had gotten so bad that I'd turned my phone off and left it in my purse or my car, anywhere that it was out of reach. I was pathetic.

"Come on. Snap out of it and come out with us. You'll feel much better."

"Where are you going?" I muttered, desperately trying to decide what I was going to do. Go out and have fun or stay home and sulk.

"Illusions. Sophie wants to check the place, out and Mila, well, she just wants to get out and party. So get yourself up! Get dressed! Put some makeup on and feel human. They will be here shortly."

IT WAS a little after ten by the time we'd finished getting ready to go out. We waited in line outside of Illusions for half an hour before finally making it to the door. The doorman checked our IDs and then let us inside. The place was packed, and the music was so loud I could barely hear myself think. I just followed Lorelai and the girls through the crowd and over to the bar.

While we waited for our drinks, I turned and looked around at the multi-layered club. It was the first time we'd been here. I scanned the room and then glanced up at the upper floors. It was dark and hard to see, but someone caught my eye. This guy stood there staring down at me. Out of the entire club, I was almost certain he was staring at me. I moved, his head moved in my direction, then I looked a little closer. I was sure it was Dylan. He was there with a few other guys, standing and looking over the ledge. I tore my eyes from him, looked around, and then glanced up again, only to see he was gone.

"Here's your drink!" Lorelai yelled in my ear as she handed me my glass.

"Let's get out of here," I yelled, following Mila and Sophie through the crowd to a spot on the dance floor.

They all began dancing and laughing while I stood there looking around. If it was him, I was certain he'd be down here after me as soon as he could be, but I hoped I was wrong.

"Loosen up!" Mila screamed. "At least look like you are having fun!" she said, coming up and wiggling against me.

Lorelai and Sophie both laughed as they joined her, dancing up against me.

I took a long sip of my drink and forced myself to start dancing. We'd danced to three or four songs and had just ordered our fourth round of drinks when I leaned over and told Lorelai I was going to the washroom.

I'd waited in line for what felt like forever, then started making my way back to my friends. I was just about there when I felt a tap on my shoulder. Turning around, I saw a man I didn't recognize smile at me. He wore an expensive-looking suit and had an earpiece in his ear. "Aurora Barlowe?"

"What?" I yelled back, not sure I heard him correctly.

This time, he leaned in closer. "Are you Aurora Barlowe?"

I nodded and smiled, feeling slightly confused. It

must have been the alcohol. He couldn't have possibly known me. I'd never seen him before.

"You and your friends have been invited up to the VIP area," he said, once again leaning into my ear.

I frowned. I didn't know what was going on. I caught sight of Lorelai watching me. She held out her hands and shrugged her shoulders, no doubt wondering what was going on. I looked at the man who wore the earpiece. "No, I think you have the wrong Aurora Barlowe."

I went to walk past him and over to the girls, but he grabbed my arm, stopping me. "I don't think I do."

I glared at the man, and the next thing I knew, Lorelai was beside me.

"Aurora, what's going on?" she questioned. "Are you okay?"

Once again, the man in the suit smiled. "The party I'm with has asked me to notify Miss Barlowe and her friends to come up to the VIP lounge. So why don't you follow me?" he said.

Lorelai looked at me and smiled. "I'll get the girls." She screamed and took off over to where they were dancing. She whispered in each of their ears and returned to us. We followed the man up to the second floor, down the hall, to a doorway covered with a curtain. Immediately, I noticed the Vancouver Dominators written on a plaque just beside the curtain and knew that my mind hadn't conjured up Dylan. He was actually here.

The man parted the curtain and waited for me to step through. Three guys I didn't recognize sat there, while Dylan leaned up against the table that held a pile of food and drinks. One look at him and I noticed his sexy smile as his eyes washed over me. He unscrewed a cap on one of the water bottles and took a drink.

"Oh, my god!" Mila screamed with excitement. "How the hell do you know these guys, Aurora? Keeping secrets from us?" she questioned with excitement.

"Aurora is full of many secrets." Lorelai winked.

I looked at my best friend and rolled my eyes.

"Ask Lorelai. You all know her brother plays for the Dominators," I said, trying to take some of the attention off me, only no one paid any attention to what I'd said.

"Hey, girls, why don't you come on over here and take a seat? We have some food on the way."

"Ladies, this is Knox Evans, Lucas Clark, and Clay Harris," Dylan said as he pushed himself off the table. "I'm Dylan Hayes." He placed his hand on the small of my back and held his other hand out to Lorelai.

Once she shook his hand, she met my eyes. I knew the look she was giving me.

"So, Aurora, how do you know these guys?" Sophie

questioned, sitting down beside Lucas and taking a bottle of beer from his hand.

"Ah, I, um… Dylan is my new stepbrother," I murmured, looking at Lorelai, who smirked.

Instantly I'd wished I could take that back.

Dylan leaned into me and whispered, "Oh, but that isn't all we could be." He pressed a kiss to my cheek.

The three guys watched and chuckled to themselves as Dylan backed up and returned to leaning on the table.

While the girls began chatting with the guys, I glanced over to see Dylan standing there watching me. I followed his eyes; they ran from my face, down my body, and back up where he met my eyes again. Then he tilted his head, signalling for me to go to him. I glanced over at my friends; they were all busy chatting it up with the guys, so I slowly backed up and made my way over to him.

"Told you I wouldn't call or text," I said, trying to prove a point.

"That's okay, the week isn't over yet." He gave me that cocky smile while grabbing a handful of nuts and shoving them into his mouth. "Still have Saturday and Sunday."

"You are impossible," I gritted.

"I may be, but I think that is what you like most

about me. So, what do you say we get out of here?" he asked, bringing his hands to my waist and pulling me between his legs.

My body was instantly on fire the moment his hands touched me.

"Not here," I murmured. I'd meant it to come out sounding like I meant what I said; however, the lack of confidence in my voice told me what I already knew.

I was his. I knew it, and I was certain he did as well.

He glanced over my shoulder and then back at me. "It's okay, they are all preoccupied."

I looked over, then back to him. "How will they get home?"

"Give your keys to one of them. If not, I will make sure that the guys make sure they all get home okay. What do you say?"

I bit my bottom lip, trying to decide what I should do: stay here with my friends or leave with him. I glanced over my shoulder to see Mila, Sophie, and Lorelai all listening to one guy share a story. They seemed to be having a good time. I knew what I wanted to do, so I turned back to Dylan and nodded.

"Where are we going?"

"You'll see. Give me your keys."

I dug into my pocket and produced my keys and handed them to him. He got up and went over to one of the guys and whispered into his ear, then handed Lorelai my car keys and whispered something to her before coming back and grabbing me by the hand, pulling me out of the VIP area. I followed him out to the parking lot, where he guided me over to his silver Mercedes and opened the passenger door for me to climb in.

"What about the girls?" I asked as he fired up the engine.

"What about them?"

"How are they getting home? I mean, they will look for me."

"No, I told Knox and your friend Lorelai to make sure he got them all home safe, and I told him you were coming with me. You're good."

He backed out of the spot and sped away before I could protest and took a sharp right turn at the end of the street.

I WAS a little afraid to be alone with Dylan after the other night. It wasn't because I was afraid of him, but more because I wanted him to do those things to me again. But to my surprise and disappointment, he was on his best behaviour. His hands hadn't drifted to my body once while we were in the car or now as we walked along the water's edge and ate pizza. He was talkative, sharing things about his dad and his childhood.

"So, how did you end up playing hockey?"

"My dad had me on skates basically the second I could walk and started me with hockey almost immediately. I loved it, so Dad just invested in me. By the time I was in my teens, I was one of the fastest on the ice, and I could handle a stick."

I couldn't help but smile.

"What's that smile for?"

My cheeks heated as he looked over at me, giving me a wink.

"You caught that." He smiled.

"What about you? What are you in school for?"

"I'm going through for the sports therapy program over at Victoria University. Lorelai as well."

"Ahhh, so I'll know someone who can fix my injuries and nurse me back to health. That's always important." He winked.

"I'm sure you already have access to those people."

"I do, but I think I like your touch a little better." He winked, once again causing me to smile and grow quiet, but the second he noticed, he started talking about hockey once again.

Soon he was sharing plays from his last game and hockey terms with me, trying to teach me a few things. When I admitted I'd never watched a hockey game, his jaw dropped.

"Like never ever?" he asked, shock lining his voice.

"Never ever."

"How can that be? I mean, Walker is your brother. He told me he watches every game."

"He does, and when he did that while we were growing up, I'd leave the room. I just never had a reason or an interest." I shrugged, wiping my mouth with a napkin and throwing it in the garbage.

"Well, I think we are immediately going to fix that. A girl of mine needs to be invested in every one of my games. Plus, I'm your interest now."

"Who says I'm your girl? I questioned as we approached his car.

"Well, think what you want, but you are my girl."

"So cocky."

He smiled and opened the car door, but said nothing while waiting for me to climb in. Once he was in the driver's seat, he sped off through the city, finally pulling into one of the newest high-rises in Vancouver. It was a building I'd always wanted to go into as well, just because of the architecture, but had never had a reason to.

"You live here?" I questioned, looking up at the tall high-rise from the passenger's seat.

He chuckled. "I do. I don't spend a substantial amount of time here, what with being on the road all the time, but it's home when I'm here and during off season. Come on."

I climbed out of the car and followed him over to the elevator. Once inside, he pressed the button for the thirty-seventh floor and the elevator shot to the top in what seemed like seconds.

"You're on the top floor?"

"Yep, I think you are going to love the view. You can see all the way to Victoria on a clear night."

He slid his key in the door and we stepped inside. He quickly flipped the lights on and waited for me to come inside before he shut and locked the door.

"Make yourself at home." He threw his keys on the kitchen counter and grabbed two beers from the fridge. "Here you go," he said, opening mine and then his.

I glanced around and slipped my feet from my shoes. The place was beautiful, decorated in beige and brown tones with pops of colour, no doubt by a decorator. It was neater than I imagined it would be for it being a guy's place. The floor-to-ceiling windows probably produced an amazing view, but the blinds were already shut. He took my hand and pulled me into the living room. The plush carpet felt nice under my bare feet as he guided me to the couch, where he sat down and patted the seat beside him.

I placed my beer on a coaster on the glass coffee table and sat down beside him, sinking into the oversized couch. I sat forward, almost afraid to touch anything.

"So, what do you think?" he asked.

"It's really nice."

The room grew quiet, and then that same unsettling feeling I got in my gut every time I'd been alone with him started again. It was as if my body and brain were having an argument. One wanted him to touch me, to take me, and the other wanted him nowhere near me. I swallowed hard, knowing he was watching me, and averted my eyes.

"Would you relax?" he said.

I looked around, my eyes burning. "I can't." I reached for my beer and took a sip before putting it back down.

Before I could turn back to face him, I felt his hand grab mine.

"It's no secret we like one another, Aurora. I know this entire situation with our parents has put a wrench in the gears for you, but you need to know that I've never felt as strong about someone before as I do about you."

"That just sounds like some sort of line to get me

into bed," I said, grabbing my beer and taking another drink.

"Well, it's not, because I've already gotten you in bed. Seriously, though, you can ask Knox."

I frowned, unsure who he was talking about. "Who's Knox?"

"The guy who was chatting with Lorelai tonight."

"He knows?" I asked, feeling my cheeks heat.

"He's one of my best friends, and he knows how bugged I was at myself for not getting your number or your name that night. He also knows how shocked and happy I was when you appeared at my dad's place."

I met his eyes. Somehow, just from looking at him, I knew now his words hadn't been a line. I'd seen plenty of guys dish out lines to Lorelai and my other friends to get what they wanted. His eyes were sincere. He'd meant what he said.

"Dylan, I…."

I paused as he slid his hand into my hair. "I meant what I said. I like you and I want a chance with you. There is nothing wrong with it, so stop thinking there is. I will not beg you."

I swallowed hard. I knew how I felt inside as well. I knew how he'd made me feel physically that night, and I knew without a doubt I wanted to feel that again. I wanted him as much as he wanted me. At least that was what my body was telling me. When I'd first seen him that night at his dad's, I think the shock set in so bad I didn't know what to do. Now, as I sat here, looking at the look on his face, in his eyes, my body was on fire. I knew what I wanted. It was him. I swallowed hard and leaned forward, my lips almost on his, so close I could feel his breath. I closed my eyes and moved the rest of the way, finally placing my lips against his.

It was the first time I'd kissed him. In fact, it was the first time I'd started a kiss with any boy. I'd always waited for them to make the move, but something inside of me wanted this so bad I couldn't wait any longer.

The second our lips touched, my mind and body forgot they were arguing and everything within me settled. Not only did he kiss me, but he grabbed me and, in one swift motion, I straddled his lap. My body was on fire as his hands gripped my ass so he could position me where he wanted.

His kiss was different this time. Slower, less demanding, and I loved how his hand snaked through my hair, holding the back of my head. I was alive with want and desire, and I wanted this to go faster, but Dylan was taking his time.

His lips left mine and travelled to my neck. He gently tugged my shirt off my shoulder and placed a kiss right where the two joined. I closed my eyes, feeling him as his lips made their way back up the column of my neck, meeting my lips once again. His hands rested on my hips, gripping the lower part of my shirt.

"Lift your arms," he murmured between kisses.

I did as he asked, and in one motion, my shirt was now on the floor.

He leaned forward, reached behind him, and pulled his shirt off, tossing it down to the floor with mine. I still couldn't get over his muscular chest as my hands rested on his pecs.

He met my eyes while his fingers pinched the clasp on my bra. When I felt the material fall away, I closed my eyes while his fingers ever so gently grazed the skin on my arms, taking my bra with them.

He leaned forward, wrapping his arms around me. He picked me up and carried me down the hall. Placing me on the floor at the foot of his bed, he pulled at the button of my jeans and removed them. He did the same with his own and then pulled me into the oversized king bed.

I lay on my back, staring up at him as he brought his lips to mine. I didn't know if it was my imagination or if tonight things felt a little different. He pulled me against him, holding me close, then rested his head down on the pillow, while my head found a home on his chest.

"I just want to hold you like this. Is that okay?" he questioned.

"Sure," I said, my voice a little strained.

I was confused. It wasn't okay. I wanted him in so many ways, I was ready.

"I don't want you to think all I want is sex. So, tonight, no sex. We'll just hold one another until we drift off."

I closed my eyes and interlocked my hand with his. Our breathing finally slowed, and hours later, I finally drifted off.

Chapter 9

Dylan

EYES TURNED our way as I followed Knox and Clay into the reception area. Tonight, we had to appear at a charity event after the game, which meant all eyes would be on us and the rest of the team.

Women eyed us as we made our way over to a table in the corner while Harris grabbed the four of us water. We all knew interviews were coming tonight, so we had to be on our best behaviour, at least until the end of the evening.

"So, you were pretty quiet about it, and I didn't want to ask, but I have to now. How did things go with Aurora the other night?" Knox questioned.

"Good." I nodded, not sure how much I should divulge with thousands of prying ears around us.

"I'm glad, you seem less on edge, and you're cleared for interviews again. Things finally settle down with all the Carlie crap?"

I shrugged. "Since we last spoke about her, I haven't heard from her, if that is what you mean."

"Good, perhaps she has finally learned her place," Clay said, shoving a small appetizer into his mouth.

"Well, what can I say? Some girls don't take a hint," Lucas added, raiding a tray of appetizers as they passed.

"She had a lot of horrible things to say online that could have destroyed your career, man," Clay added.

I nodded. "Yep, and that is why public relations and my lawyer have been watching for the next bomb to drop. When they suggested sending the cease and desist, I doubted it would work. I was wrong. I just am afraid she is waiting and calculating when to make a move."

"She'd be stupid to do that. Wouldn't she?" Knox questioned.

"She would be, considering. I've stayed out of the news just like asked. Tonight will be my first appearance since it all went down. To say I'm a little nervous is an understatement."

"Maybe you shouldn't have broken things off with her?" Clay said, swiping more appetizers from the bar.

"You know why he did," Knox added, looking my direction.

I knew what he was hinting at, but the truth was Carlie and I were over long before we'd actually broken up. He knew it, as did the rest of the guys. She didn't need to take our breakup public, especially when the entire breakup was her fault. However, she tried to make me look like I was the bad guy. She took our already public breakup far more public and made claims about me online, but the images she'd attached to the article were a lie. It was from a game three weeks prior to the date she'd claimed. I'd come out of a bar with a bunch of fans, and I had my arm wrapped around some girl. She claimed I cheated. It was humiliating and brought a ton of terrible publicity my way.

"Does she know about the trip to Cozumel and Aurora?"

I shrugged. "Do I care?"

"You might if she catches wind of it."

"Look, Cozumel, has nothing to do with her. It was over eight months after we called it quits. If she is jealous, let her be jealous. She made her bed. Now, can we drop this topic? It's like asking for bad karma."

"Yeah, you are right. Especially right before your

first interview in over a year," Knox said, smacking me on the shoulder.

It was then I felt my cell phone vibrate in my pocket, and I reached in to see a message from Aurora. I stepped away from the table and quickly sent a text back. It had been three weeks since the night Aurora finally admitted to herself and to me she wanted me. We'd spent a wonderful night together before I'd had to leave for a series of games in Florida. She'd gone back to Victoria for classes, and since then, our schedules had been near impossible to sync, so not only had we not seen one another, we'd barely spoken. I'd been trying to fix that. I'd texted her prior to the game and again after, and finally just now she was responding.

Dylan: What are you doing tonight?

Aurora: Lorelai and I are studying for finals.

Dylan: So does that mean you didn't see the game?

Aurora: Sadly not. We have to pass this exam or we can kiss our meeting with the head of the Therapy Department with the Dominators good-bye.

Dylan: Do I need to remind you that not only do you have Lorelai's brother rooting for you, but you have me? If he can't make it happen, then I'll make sure the pair of you still get the interview.

Aurora: How are you going to do that?

Dylan: I have my ways. I'm a very persuasive individual. ;)

Aurora: Don't need to remind me of that. However, you promised not to get involved.

Dylan: I did?

I SMILED as I watched those three little dots bounce around.

Aurora: You did. ;P

Dylan: and you promised you'd watch the game tonight.

Aurora: Sigh...I know *buries face in hands*

Dylan: You already know you're going to kill the test.

Aurora: Thanks for the vote of confidence. I guess you'll have to kidnap me and make me watch one live.

Dylan: Deal. I'll call you in the morning. It will be a late night tonight. Charity function. They are waiting for me for my interview.

Aurora: Okay. Talk to you tomorrow. Have a good night.

Dylan: You too.

I POCKETED my phone just as Knox returned from speaking with the press.

"You're up there, Hayes."

I nodded, feeling a little nervous as I walked over to where they were interviewing. They asked the standard questions about the game and about the charity. I figured we were through when the woman turned to me and surprised me by telling me she had a couple more questions to ask.

"So, Dylan, you've been out of the spotlight for a

bit. Your fans have missed you. There are many questions they have, most circling about your personal life. They want to know where you have been?"

I'd specifically been told that the only questions they'd be asking were the ones approved by our PR team. I glanced over my shoulder to see if I could find any PR person, but no one was in sight.

"I've been here. Just took a break from interviews," I said, saying exactly what the PR department had told me to say if I was ever asked.

"There have been a lot of rumours about your personal life. Many want to know about your romantic life. What happened with Carlie?"

Again, I smiled. I knew they would be after information on what had happened regarding Carlie and me.

"I decline to answer," I said, going to walk away.

"There is more."

"What would they like to know?"

The interviewer smiled. "Well, the crucial question is, are you seeing anyone?"

"I really don't have a comment about that. Aside from there is someone I have my eyes on," I said, waving to the camera. "I have to be going now. I have a speech to make," I said, stepping away from the interviewer and the camera.

I didn't know how that interview would go down or

what kind of backlash I'd get from Carlie once it came out, so I immediately headed over to the first PR person I saw and pulled her aside.

"I SAW YOUR INTERVIEW."

I couldn't tell from the tone of her voice if she was angry or impressed with my answer to who I was seeing. So, I played it safe.

"Oh?"

"So, who do you have your eye on? Someone I should be worried about?"

I was almost certain there was a hint of a smile in her voice. At least I hoped my ears weren't deceiving me.

"Only if you are worried about yourself."

The line went quiet for a bit. I wanted her to say something; I wanted to know she wanted me as much as I wanted her, and just when I thought she wasn't going to say anything at all, she surprised me.

"What time does your flight come in?"

I could hear the curiosity in her voice, along with the nerves. Her voice shook as she asked that question, which I thought was the cutest.

"Why? Are you excited to see me? Have you been missing me?"

Again, the line went quiet. I could hear her breathing and knew she was probably debating answering me.

"What if I am?" she asked, her voice quieter this time.

"I'd be thrilled to know it."

I lay in bed, the comforter draped at my waist as I waited for her to speak. My cock had been semi hard since I'd heard her voice on the other line.

"Well, I'd be lying if I said I wasn't a little excited to see you."

"Does that mean I'm finally growing on you?"

"You grew on me the first night I met you."

Her voice shook with that admission, and it turned me on more than anything. The fact she was nervous about sharing these things with me made me wonder how she must have felt that first night. I could already tell that she really wasn't the girl she'd portrayed that night. I was probably the only risk she'd ever taken in her entire life, and I guessed that for months afterward she probably kicked herself for doing something stupid.

"What made you sleep with me in Mexico?" I questioned. I wanted to know the truth.

She sighed. "I'm not sure I want to tell you."

"Why not? You clearly had no clue who I was, so I don't think it was for bragging rights."

"No."

"Then what was it?"

"Oh god. It was stupid. I…I'd just broken up with my boyfriend and wanted to reclaim myself. I was on a mission, and I'd just about given up when you met me at the end of the walkway. It was more self-destruction than anything. It's not something I normally do."

"Ah, so you're telling me I was a get over him fuck? I see how it is. I feel so used."

Aurora giggled. "That's what it started out as, but that isn't what it is now."

"I see, and what is it now?" The line went silent, and I waited. "Are you there?"

"Yeah, I'm here. I don't really know what this is now. I know I'm attracted to you and that I like spending time with you, but I have no clue what this really is or what you even want. Guess you could say I'm a little confused."

I thought for a moment. I wanted her to know I wanted more than just sex, which was pretty much all we'd done every time we'd gotten together, aside from that one night at my apartment.

"What I want is a date. That is what I really want. I know how I feel about you on the physical level. I want to see if there is more."

"So, what time does your flight get in? Or are you going to make me stalk all arrivals?"

"Is that a yes?"

"Yes."

I smiled to myself. "I should be home by two. I'm home for two days and then back on the road."

"I write an exam tomorrow morning. Then I am free for a couple of days. Lorelai has family plans, and I have to drop her at her brother's place, so I can meet you at your place. We could have our date then."

I closed my eyes, excitement building at the thought of being able to see her again.

"Doesn't give me much time to plan anything, but to be honest, I can't fucking wait. It's been too long."

I reached down under the blankets and gripped my cock. I was hard just thinking about getting to spend time with her.

"It has," she said breathlessly.

The line went quiet as I slowly stroked my cock, thinking of her lips on me. God, I'd never felt this way with Carlie, which only solidified that she had been the wrong girl for me. Every time I thought of Aurora, this was what happened.

"What are you doing over there?" I asked, curious to know.

The line was quiet for a moment.

"Lying in bed, thinking about you. What about you?"

The tone of her voice had changed, making me even harder. I slowly stoked myself, imagining her hand in place of mine.

"The same." I swallowed hard. "Are you…touching…"

"Mmmm…what if I am?"

"Fuck, I wish I could watch…" I whispered, closing my eyes.

"Isn't that a little forward? I mean, all you said you wanted was a date." She giggled.

"Okay, perhaps I want what we have going on now *and* a date."

A loud knock on my door made me jump, then I heard Knox and Clay yelling my name. Then laughter came through the door, and I knew they were both drunk. I closed my eyes and let out the breath I was holding.

"Fuck," I muttered under my breath.

"What is it?" she questioned, the tone of her voice going from low and sexy to panicked.

Throwing the covers off me and slipping on my boxers, I got up from the bed, pissed that we'd been interrupted. I'd dreamt of talking to her like this, and now here we were, and these idiots had to interrupt us.

"Dylan? What is going on?" she questioned.

"The boys are here," I said, annoyance filling my voice. "I've got to go. Can I call you later?"

"Yep. I'll try to wait up for a bit, otherwise, see you tomorrow?"

As I pulled the door open, Knox and Clay fell into the room laughing, each with a beer in their hands. It looked like the party had continued well after I'd left.

"Yeah, just remember where we left off, okay?" I said, before ending the call.

Chapter 10

Aurora

I'D BARELY BEEN able to contain my excitement all day. It had been a struggle to get through the exam, but once I'd finished, we raced home and got ready for some time off. The ferry ride felt like it took forever, but now I sat in the car out front of her brother's house waiting while Lorelai pulled her things from the car.

"Have a good time. If you need me, just text and I'll come get you early if needed," I told Lorelai as she pulled the last bag from the back seat.

Lorelai was helping her brother and Candace with wedding plans for the weekend, and since her brother Phil was best friends with her ex, Hugo, and he was in the wedding party, I wanted her to make sure she knew she had an out if she needed.

"Thanks, but Candace promised me he wouldn't be there this weekend. She's been trying to talk Phil out of having him in the wedding party too. She says it's not fair to me after we broke up to allow him to be part of the family. I just hope she can convince him. God, could you imagine how horrific that would be, being stuck on a tiny island with him?"

"Hawaii isn't that tiny," I said, checking my phone for messages.

"Ha, says you. It is very tiny if your ex is on it with you. Believe me."

"Hey, just remember you hold the power, my dear. He dumped you, remember?"

"I know. Doesn't mean I want to see him soon. I especially don't want to see him with someone else when I'm single. Phil told Candace he's apparently bringing someone."

I frowned. "The invites haven't even gone out yet. How does he know he's even allowed to bring a plus one?"

I got out of the car and hugged my best friend. "I get it. Breathe and have a good time," I said as I made my way around to the driver's side and climbed back in the car.

"Where are you going to be?"

"Dylan's," I said, my stomach flipping with butterflies.

The butterfly feeling started when we'd gotten off the phone last night. I couldn't stop wondering where that conversation was going to go when we'd been so rudely interrupted. However, thinking back, I was glad nothing had happened. I'd never had phone sex before.

"So you didn't tell your mother you were coming to Vancouver?"

I shook my head. "I haven't spoken to her. I'm almost positive that she and Joe are still on their honeymoon in Europe, anyway."

"Alright, well, have fun. I'll call if I need."

I waved and looked toward the house to see Candace step out onto the front porch. I waved, said good-bye to Lorelai once more, and then pulled away from the curb. I made my way through Vancouver, finally pulling into the parking lot of Dylan's building. I glanced around and noticed his car parked in his spot, so I pulled into the visitors' section and parked in the only available spot and made my way inside.

I stood outside his door, a small duffel bag in my hand, while my other hand shook as I knocked and then waited. I was about to knock again when the door opened and a soaking wet Dylan stood before me with a towel wrapped around his waist. Almost immediately, my mouth went dry as my eyes travelled down his built chest to his abs, to that delicious vee that was peeking out just above the band of the towel.

"Wow…" I muttered under my breath at the sight in front of me.

He glanced down at himself and then looked at me with that stupid cocky smile he always wore, the one I'd been dying to see again.

"Get in here," he said, gripping my wrist and pulling me inside and into his arms.

Instantly, his lips were against mine as he pried the bag from my hand while his other held onto the towel that was wrapped at his waist. Once my bag had fallen to the floor, he took hold of my hand and pulled me down the hall to the bathroom where the shower was still running and dropped his towel. He pulled at my shirt, popping button by button, and then shoved my shirt from my shoulders. He pulled at the button on my jeans. Want coursed through my veins as he pushed them down my legs.

I stood there half undressed, breathing hard as he grinned at me, turned, and stepped into the shower, leaving the door open.

"You coming?"

"Did you plan this?" I questioned, stepping out of my pants that were bunched at my ankles.

When I'd pulled away from the curb, I'd messaged

him to let him know I was on my way. That notice would have given him plenty of time to get himself into the shower.

"I'll leave that question for you to figure out." He chuckled.

Seconds later, I stood under the hot water, my back pressed up against the wall of his shower, his body pressed against mine as he took my mouth with his. His kiss was frantic at first, then it slowed. He wrapped me in his arms, kissing me slow and deep, his tongue washing through my mouth as he pulled me tighter against him.

"I missed you," he murmured between kisses. "I thought about this all night last night."

"Me too," I said, panting.

"What were you doing on the phone last night while we were talking?" he questioned, moving to my neck, kissing his way from my ear to where my shoulder met my neck.

"Wouldn't you like to know?" I giggled, then sucked in a breath as he brought his lips to the top of my breasts.

He stopped what he was doing and placed his hands on the shower wall on either side of my head and met my eyes. "I would."

The intensity in his eyes made me weak in the knees as he stared at me, waiting for me to tell him what it was he already knew. With my heart in my throat, I closed my eyes and jumped a little when I felt his hand graze the front of my thigh. My body shook as he trailed his finger up my inner thigh.

"Were you touching yourself?" he whispered, his breath tickling my ear. "I had my cock in my hand, thinking of you."

Fire flooded my body as his fingers found their way to my centre, and I let out a moan as he gently ran them over my clit. I opened my eyes to see him watching me.

"You like that?" he questioned.

Before I could answer him, he licked his lips and devoured my mouth with his.

WE SAT in a quiet corner out on the balcony of The Sunset, an upscale Italian restaurant on the water's edge. I poured us both another glass of wine while we waited for dessert to arrive.

I'd planned this date from my hotel room almost as soon as I'd hung up the phone from talking with her. I'd scoured the internet looking for restaurants in the area that I thought would be a good choice. When I came up empty-handed, I pulled Knox aside and asked him. This had always been his go-to place, and to be honest, he wasn't wrong. It was perfect. Watching the sunset over the water during dinner was probably the most romantic part of the night and, she admitted it to me as the sky went from shades of pink to hues of purple.

We talked about everything under the sun. Food, music, hobbies, her childhood and mine. She picked up her wineglass and brought it to her perfect full lips.

"Alright, I have a question. What are the little things that improve your days?"

"When I need a pick-me-up or having a tough day, I always go for the cinnamon scones at Sip and Stir. What about you?"

"Probably skating. I just get out on the ice and go. It always takes my mind off everything."

"What is one quality you wish you had?"

"Oh god, that is tough."

"No, it's not."

She brought her fingers to her lips. "I wish I could be more like Lorelai at times. She just has a way of reading people, and I've always admired it. What about you?"

"Sometimes, I wish I could be more like Knox in the relationship department. He's just so easygoing, where I'm more the relationship type guy."

"Nothing wrong with the way you are," she whispered.

I met her eyes and smiled. "Okay, I have another. If you could relive one day, what would it be?"

A light blush rose to her cheeks, and she averted her eyes down to the glass she was holding. I sat there waiting for her answer when she finally spoke.

"Are you going to tell me what is in the bag?" she questioned, looking over with curiosity. She'd been eyeing the bag the entire night.

"Once you answer the question, you can look in the bag," I said.

"Do you want an honest answer?"

"Uh, yeah, the whole point of tonight is to get to know one another on a better basis. So, the truth would be preferable."

She spun the stem of the glass between her fingers. Keeping her head down, she muttered something to herself.

"I didn't quite catch that," I said, reaching across the table and placing my hand on top of hers.

She looked up at me. "You're probably going to laugh."

"Doubt it."

"Okay, here goes nothing. The one night I wish I could relive would have been that night in Mexico with you."

I didn't know what to say as her eyes met mine, but somehow her answer warmed me.

"Why that night?" I asked, my heart beating a little harder.

"There would be things I'd change. First, I'd have gotten your name so I didn't need to wait so long to find you again," she whispered.

I reached down beside me and grabbed the bag, handing it to her. "I hope you like it. I was debating not giving it to you for fear you thought I was being a little too possessive."

She looked at me with curious eyes then opened the bag.

"It's my jersey," I said, as she pulled it out of the bag.

A smile fell over her lips as she flipped it around to see my name across the back. "Thank you. I love it."

"So you'll wear it?"

She nodded. "I will."

AFTER DINNER, we made our way over to a private nightclub where we were meeting up with Clay and Knox.

Once inside, Dylan ordered us each a drink from the bar and we headed out to the dance floor. Dylan took a moment to text them both to tell them where we were, then we started dancing.

Once Clay and Knox arrived, they came over and said hello then made their way to the bar. We were going to follow, but a slow song came on. Dylan grabbed my hand and pulled me against him. Resting my head against his shoulder.

As the music played, we swayed together. Something about this moment made me wish it would never end. I felt him press a kiss to my forehead as he held me in his arms. I'd just closed my eyes and relaxed in his arms when I felt someone grab hold of my hair and pull me backward, ripping me away from Dylan. I tried to fight, but there was nothing I could do, I couldn't see who it was.

The room spun as I fell backward, until whoever it was finally let me go. I tried to catch myself before I fell to the ground but didn't succeed. I blinked a few times and tried to focus before I moved. I got up on my knees and turned to see a woman about my age shouting at Dylan. I couldn't make out what she was saying, but watched in horror as she smacked him across the face. She then began shouting at him again, only his time, she pointed at me.

Dylan came over to where I sat on the ground and

grabbed my hands, bringing me up to my feet as she continued to shout at him.

"You asshole. Is this the piece of ass you have your eye on?" she screamed as she pointed in my direction.

Clay and Knox both came over to us and pulled me back away from her, stepping in front of me to protect me. The three of us stood there watching the events unfold before us.

"Carlie, it's over," Dylan gritted, wiping at the spilled drink that was all over his shirt. "It's been over for a long fucking time."

"Please…we had plans," she cried.

Dylan shook his head and glanced over at me. Shock, hurt, and anger flooded me as I watched him stand there wiping the drink from his shirt. This girl looked absolutely gutted.

"You can't give up on us that easily." She sniffled.

Dylan shook his head. "Carlie, there isn't anything left!"

"I made mistakes, Dylan. You were right. I didn't know what I had with you, but I do now, and I don't want to live my life with a huge regret. I need you back in my life. We were talking about getting married and starting a family. Settling down," she cried.

My stomach churned and the room spun. I glanced at Knox and Clay, who stood there, neither of them looking surprised. This seemed to be something that was a common occurrence for them. As the events of the past few minutes ran through my mind, my hearing became fuzzy. Never in my life had I been *the other woman,* and it made me sick to my stomach to think that's what this was.

"Carlie, I told you, we are over. If you never got the hint from the last letter from my lawyer, then I don't know what it's going to take," Dylan said, coming over to me and wrapping his arm around me.

Carlie spun around and glared at me, then at Dylan.

"Dylan, don't do this…" she sobbed. "And you… you slut…you stole him from me," she sneered, raising her fist.

Dylan grabbed me and ripped me from the spot where I stood, Clay and Knox both staying there protecting the pair of us as we left the club. Once outside, we all walked in silence, Clay and Knox keeping an eye out from behind us as we made our way through the parking lot to Dylan's car.

My heart pounded in my chest as the events that had just unfolded before my eyes replayed in my mind. I didn't know what to think. What I knew was I wanted to get away from this place and from Dylan as quickly as I could. He opened the door and turned to me, waiting for me to get inside.

I swallowed hard as I looked at the three of them,

my stomach rolling. Why wasn't anyone explaining anything? Who was that girl? Was Dylan married? Was he in a relationship that I didn't know about? I had so many questions, and the world seemed to be moving at such a fast pace right now, I didn't know what to do or what to ask.

"Come on, let's go," Dylan said, waiting for me to get in.

I shook my head and slowly stepped back away from the car. "Not until you tell me what that was about," I said, standing my ground while trying to fight back tears.

"Not here," Dylan said, still waiting for me to get in the car.

I shook my head and stepped back.

"Come on, Aurora, get in," Dylan demanded. "We have to get out of here before she comes out."

When I didn't move, Knox stepped forward. "Come on, he'll explain once you're in the car."

I shook my head and pulled my cell phone from my back pocket, quickly dialing Lorelai. If she didn't answer or if she or her brother couldn't come to get me, I'd get into a cab and head to her brother's place. I didn't care, right now. I wanted to be anywhere but here. If he wanted me to stay, then I wanted to know what that entire situation was about and he'd better start explaining.

Chapter 11

Dylan

"COME ON, Aurora, just get in the car and give me a chance to explain. Please hang up the phone and just hear me out," I pleaded, reaching to take her phone from her hand.

She glared at me as she ripped her hand away and shook her head. "I can't hang up now. Lorelai will worry something is wrong."

"Just hang up the phone and get in the car," I said, clenching my fists.

There was no telling what Carlie would do if she came over here. There was also no knowing if there were reporters inside the club either, or, for that matter, outside. I had to get out of here, not only to protect myself, but to protect Aurora. She'd never be able to deal with a group of swarming reporters.

She looked at me and then down at her phone, finally ending the call, shoving it into her back pocket.

"You didn't win, just so you know. She wasn't answering." She crossed her arms in front of her.

It was then I heard my name being called, and I glanced over my shoulder in time to see Carlie step out the back door of the bar looking around for me.

"We'll take care of it," Knox said, pulling his phone out.

"Just call our lawyer and the police," I said.

"On it." Knox and Clay took off toward the back door of the bar together, leaving Aurora and me alone. Since I'd had issues with this girl before, a phone call to the police was all it was going to take. That and to my lawyer, which Knox was on top of so I could get out of here. It was then Aurora's phone rang, and she pulled it from her back pocket and looked at the screen.

"Don't answer it. Please. I'm begging you to give me a chance to explain," I pleaded.

Aurora met my eyes and looked down at her phone, biting her bottom lip. "I've got to answer it. It's Lorelai. She'll worry if I don't," she said, bringing the phone to her ear.

"Hey," she sang, sounding like there was nothing wrong.

She listened as she stared at me, while I continued to plead with my eyes that she'd give me the opportunity to explain my side of this nightmare. I watched as she listened. I couldn't read her. I didn't know what it was she was going to say. I just hoped it was what I wanted her to do.

"Oh goodness, Lorelai, no, everything is fine. I must have butt dialed you while I was in the club," she said, meeting my eyes. "No, everything is fine."

At those words, the fear of losing her left me, at least for now. At least I knew I still had time to explain my side of the story. After, if she wanted to leave, I'd have to let her, but I prayed she didn't. I didn't want to lose her already, especially not this way.

"No really, I'm sorry. I promise everything is okay. I know Phil will come if I need, but really it was only an accident. I didn't even feel my phone vibrate or hear it ring until I got outside. I'll call in the morning. Again, I'm sorry for scaring you. Okay, you too, have fun."

I watched as she ended the call, and then she pocketed her phone and looked up at me, crossing her arms. Her eyes held so many questions, and I hoped I could answer them all.

"Well? Now is your chance."

I nodded toward the car. "Get in. I'll explain when we are back at the apartment."

"This is ridiculous," she grumbled as she shoved past me and climbed into my car.

AURORA STOOD before me as I sat on the couch in my living room. The drive back was silent, neither of us saying a word. I imagined that had driven her crazy to be quiet the entire time when I knew she'd wanted me to explain everything to her in the parking lot back there.

I sat on the couch as she paced in front of me. I was trying to decide where to start—the beginning, the middle or the end—but each time I looked at her, all I saw was impatience and irritation lining her pretty face as she stood there waiting for me to begin.

"We've been back here for twenty minutes and I'm still waiting. You can't force me to stay here, you know. I can always head down to my car and go to Lorelai's," she said, crossing her arms in front of her.

I clenched my jaw tight. I was still fuming from earlier, and I didn't need the attitude from her right now. What I needed was patience and understanding, something I rarely, if ever, received from Carlie. However, I had to remember that I hadn't given her the story yet to receive any sort of understanding.

I glanced up at her. I could see the anger in her eyes and in her body language. She had every right to be angry. Carlie had almost ripped the hair right out of her head.

I'd already heard from Knox and Clay. They'd called the police and our lawyer, but Carlie had taken off before anyone got there.

"I'm waiting, and I'm giving you another twenty seconds to start before I put my shoes on and walk out that door for good."

"Alright, look, first, are you alright? Do you hurt anywhere?" I asked, getting up and making my way over to her. As soon as I went to place my hands on her arms, she stepped out of my reach.

"I'll be fine. What the hell was that? Who was that?"

"That was my ex."

Aurora said nothing. She just looked at me, waiting for me to continue.

"It started with Sullivan Novak," I said, anger coursing through my body as she watched me. It didn't matter how many times I'd told the story. His name still made me want to punch anything in my way, just as much as it did when we played against him and his team.

"Who is that?"

"He was a guy on our team. The team traded him midway through last season, shortly before everything went down, thank god, otherwise he probably wouldn't be alive, and or I'd be in jail."

"Okay."

"Carlie made advances toward him, or maybe I should say he made advances toward her, I'm not entirely sure. I found out about them at an away game when I'd thought she was away with her family. When I was on my way back to my hotel room, I heard what sounded like her voice. I turned to look, and that was when I saw her with him. They were kissing, and then they entered his hotel room and shut the door.

"Anger filled me, so I marched down the hall and banged on the door. She answered, then burst into tears, begging me to forgive her. She'd apparently been sexting with him for months and had been seeing him behind my back. Every chance she got, she was in bed with him, every family vacation she'd lied about, every work trip she'd gone on and each time he was in town and told me she couldn't watch or come to the game she'd been with him. They'd done this right under my nose after lying to me. When I found out, it fucking gutted me. My world stopped."

Aurora said nothing. I wasn't sure what to think at this point as she stared at me.

"It didn't stop there. When I stood my ground, she dragged my name through the mud every chance she got. Our breakup was already all over online and in the papers. Reporters ate the story up. Then she started dragging my name right through the mud on social media and to reporters every chance she got. It came to the point I had to get a cease and desist, and a restraining order put in place. She was ruining me. I lost sponsors because of her. She was literally killing my career and my bank account."

"She didn't seem to think you were over tonight. She seemed to—"

I stopped where she was going with this, because it was something I'd heard repeatedly every time she surfaced and acted this way. "Let me guess, it looks like I caused the breakup, right? Like I was the one who cheated. If you were to dig hard enough, you could probably find an old article online that says the same thing, but I can assure you it was her actions that landed her where she is. I cut her loose so she could have what she wanted, Sullivan Novak. Other than that, none of it was me.

"Also, we weren't engaged. We'd talked about getting married, about having kids, but that was all. There was nothing in the works. To be honest, I wasn't even sure she was the one. I'd started having doubts about five months earlier. All she did was confirm it. After, there was no room for forgiveness after what happened. She went for the other guy and tried to blame me for it all."

"I'm just telling you what I saw. She attacked me as if she were still with you and I were your latest conquest."

"Of course she did, and honestly, I was expecting this when I did that interview the other night. It was stupid of me to even answer the question they asked about my personal relationship. I should have known better. I should have known that wasn't an approved question."

"Approved questions?"

"Yes, the interviewers are supposed to give our PR department a list of questions and they go through and approve of them. I haven't been interviewed in months because of her, but my lawyers and the team's lawyers said things should be fine now. I was told all questions were approved, but I'm guessing they snuck that one in and that our PR department never got a copy of some of those questions. Without being warned, they caught me on the spot. I just couldn't pass over it."

"So you are saying she only did this because of that interview?"

"That's my guess. She hasn't been around otherwise."

"So you're not dating her? Right?"

"No, and I'm not interested. I wish she'd just leave me the hell alone, because who the hell knows what will come out about this tomorrow?"

"Tomorrow?"

"Yes, everything snowballs in this business, especially with the media. So, if there were any media outlets nearby, this will be all over the place in the morning."

Aurora turned away from me, walked over to the window, and looked out over the city. She was quiet, and I was worried as she stood there thinking. The last thing I wanted was for her to leave. I wanted her to stay and be with me tonight. I hadn't planned for the night to go this way, and I'd be back on the road soon enough. Trying to navigate through this problem without being near her would be next to impossible. We were too new to one another to even try.

With my head down, I walked over to her. This time when I reached out, she stood there as I placed my hands on her arms. She looked up at me, her eyes unsure.

"I swear to you, if you are lying to me…"

"I'm not. I wouldn't do that."

She studied me, not breaking eye contact for a second.

"How do I know I'm not just some rebound?"

I pulled her against my chest and wrapped my arms around her. "I couldn't have done that. I'm not that type. I'm a one-woman guy. As angry as I was over everything that happened, I was also gutted and needed time to make sure that I didn't hurt someone in the process of healing. During that time, I stayed single for over a year. I couldn't get involved right away, I was hurting, and I swore to myself I wouldn't bring that into another relationship.

"I don't know how much of this to believe. You're a guy. Guys don't normally care, and I'm sure you had many opportunities of girls dropping at your feet."

"That's fair, and you're right, there were plenty of opportunities, but I'm not that type. You can ask Knox."

She looked up at me. I could see she was searching my eyes for answers, to see if what I was saying was the truth.

"I don't know, Dylan." She averted her eyes from mine again.

"I promise you, I'm telling you the truth," I said, my voice low.

This time when her eyes met mine, I didn't hesitate. I placed my hand on her cheek and brought my lips to hers.

"Stop, just stop." She pushed at my chest and stepping away from me.

"What?" I questioned.

"This is too much, Dylan. I don't know what the hell to believe."

"I'm telling you."

She stepped away from me and started toward the door.

"I know, but...I think I just need some space," she said, turning back to me.

I looked at her; she glanced at her shoes, then back at me. If she wanted to leave there was nothing I could do. She looked back at me, then at her keys that lay beside her purse, then she sighed.

"Can I at least take a hot bath and just have some time to myself?"

Relief ran over me. She didn't want to leave. I nodded. You can find towels in the bathroom closet. Take your time. There are Epsom salts under the counter if you want them, and the TV remote is on the wall just beside the lightswitch.

I LAY IN BED, my arms behind my head, staring up at the ceiling. It was a little after two. Aurora lay beside me, curled up on her side. She'd taken a hot bath while I talked with Knox. When she hadn't returned to the living room an hour later, I wandered down the hall to find her curled up on my bed, sound asleep. I covered her and eventually came to bed.

I shifted, trying again to get comfortable.

"You awake?" she asked, her voice barely audible.

"Yeah. Is every okay?"

She shifted under the covers and rolled over, facing me. She lay there, studying my face for a bit, and then slid her hand into mine. "Don't get mad, but I was worried that maybe I was just another proverbial notch on your belt."

I rolled onto my side; her face bathed with the moonlight that poured through the sheer curtains.

"I'm sorry if I got angry."

She wiggled her way a little closer, pressing her lips against mine, her hand resting on my side. I reached out, pulling her closer to me. She was wearing a set of boy shorts and a tank top that left hardly anything to my imagination.

"It's okay," I whispered, raising myself up on my forearm. I brought my lips to hers and kissed her slowly as my hand found its place on her hip. As my tongue washed through her mouth, I tugged on the drawstring of her boy shorts, and she lifted just enough that I could slide them off her. I threw them over my head before rolling over to grab a condom from the bedside drawer. When I turned back, Aurora lay there, completely naked, biting her bottom lip. Even though the room was dark, I could still see the light-pink blush on her cheeks in the moonlight as I kissed her hard.

I rolled onto my back and ripped open the condom, rolling it on me. When I went to roll back over, she surprised me by pressing her hand to my chest. She kissed my lips and threw her leg over me, straddling my lap.

"Is this okay?" she questioned quietly, almost as if she were ashamed by being so forward.

I couldn't help but chuckle. "Of course. No complaints from this guy," I said, brushing her hair back out of her face and tasting her lips again.

Chapter 12

Aurora

"COME WITH ME," Dylan said, taking hold of my hands.

He'd woken me up with a cup of coffee in bed, then he'd given me a few minutes to get dressed, and when he returned, he held a black tie which he covered my eyes with and tied it at the back of my head.

"Trust me," he whispered as he led me out of the bedroom. "You're fine, just keep walking…stop…step down…okay, and keep walking…"

I could already feel a breeze on my face.

"Where are we going?" I questioned.

"Just a few more steps….and now, you can look."

I felt him reach behind me and pull the tie, letting it fall away from my eyes. A smile fell to my lips to see the table on his screened-in balcony set.

"What's this?"

"Sunday morning breakfast," he said, pulling the chair out for me, waiting for me to sit down.

He poured us each a glass of orange juice and then headed inside, returning with two amazing looking omelets.

"When did you do this?" I asked, shocked.

"While you were sleeping." He pressed a kiss to the top of my head.

He sat down across from me, and we dug into the omelets.

I closed my eyes as I put the first bite into my mouth. "God that is great," I muttered.

Dylan chuckled. "I'm glad."

"What?" I questioned looking over at him.

"You like the omelet." He winked. "Only wish I'd of had that same effect on you last night."

I could feel my cheeks heat.

"Or did I have that effect on you last night?"

He leaned back against his chair and looked over at me, his eyes saying everything.

"I think you know exactly what effect you had on me last night. You just want me to confirm it."

"So what if I do?"

I couldn't tear my eyes from his. There was something so damn sexy about him. He scooted forward on his chair and leaned in, taking my mouth with his.

"What about breakfast?" I asked breathlessly as he kissed his way down my neck.

"The only breakfast I want right now is you," he said, picking me up off the ground and carrying me inside.

I GRABBED two coffees from Sip and Stir and headed out the front door, taking a seat on the bench just outside the coffeehouse. I glanced at my watch. I'd come to Vancouver to do a bunch of shopping, and about an hour ago my mother called, asking me to meet her. I hurried, and now I sat waiting; she was late, as usual. It shouldn't have surprised me, but it did, since she was the one who'd called me.

I pulled my phone from my back pocket to see if Dylan had messaged, only to have a heavy feeling of disappointment follow when I saw there was nothing there.

"Aurora!" I heard my mother call.

I looked up and saw her walking toward me, waving. She was wearing a white pantsuit with a bright-green shirt underneath. She looked radiant, more so than I'd ever seen.

"Hey, Penelope," I called, standing up. She wrapped her arms around me and then placed a kiss on my cheek.

"So good to see you, sweetie. Thanks for meeting me."

"Of course, and I got you a coffee," I said, holding up the cup for her to take.

She smiled. "Thanks, now let's walk. Shall we?"

We headed across the street and into the park.

"How was the honeymoon?"

"Fantastic, Aurora. If you ever get a chance, you need to go to Europe. We ate in so many amazing places. We visited the Louvre, we dined in the Eiffel tower, we strolled through Luxembourg Gardens. Then we headed to Barcelona and finished the month in Prague."

I'd never known my mother to be interested in travel, never mind to any of the places she'd just mentioned. It still shocked me that, almost overnight, Penelope had become an entirely different person. Never mind that she had called and asked to see me. I couldn't in my entire life remember a time that she was interested in anything Walker, or I ever did.

"So, why did you want to see me?" I questioned.

"Can't your mother want to spend time with you?"

"Of course," I replied.

"Okay then. I just wanted to check in with you, see how school was going."

I frowned, unsure of why she was even asking. I felt like I was living in some sort of alternate universe.

"Good, only a couple more months and I'll have my degree."

"How was your last exam? I ran into Lorelai's mother. She said that you two are studying harder than ever."

"Yep, we get our grades back for that exam tomorrow, but things are looking amazing."

"Have I told you how proud I am of you? You wanted something, and you reached out and took control. Something that I've failed to do during my life."

My mother was such a free spirit, it was strange to hear her talking like this. Maybe Lorelai was right and Joe had been a good choice for her, but this was still weird to me. Or was she sick? Panic flooded me for a moment, then quickly passed. She wasn't sick, maybe lovesick, but not actually sick.

Just then I felt my phone vibrate in my pocket and I pulled it out in time to see Dylan's name flash on the screen. I was still feeling confused about the other night and really wanted advice from someone. Then I caught my mother smiling at me.

"Mom, can I…talk to you about something?" I questioned.

My mom stopped walking and turned to me, an odd look coming over her face. I could recall one other time I'd actually called her Mom in the past few years. It was always Penelope to her face, except for when I'd panicked at Joe's house because Dylan had been there. She was fine with it. Penelope said she actually preferred being called by her actual name instead of mom. She said it made her feel younger.

"Is everything okay?" she asked, taking a seat on a park bench and tapping the space beside her.

I sat down beside her and looked out over the park, not sure how to answer that. Was everything alright? I supposed so. I was more confused than anything.

"Mom, I want to ask you about relationships."

My mother perked up. "Alright, what would you like to know?"

I thought for a moment. She probably wasn't the right person to ask, or maybe she was because she'd had tons of relationships, but what I wanted was sound advice, not Penelope's flighty wisdom.

I continued to sit there, thinking about how to ask what I wanted to know, when she patted my leg and leaned back against the bench seat.

"Does this advice you need have anything to do with Dylan?"

I bit my bottom lip and nodded. "It's weird to me still, but I don't know what we are to one another. I don't know how to tell if this is something serious, or something I shouldn't invest my time in."

I'd been in one relationship, or what I would have called a relationship, with Greg. Other than that, I'd had the occasional date, but none of them ever went anywhere. I'd also always invested way more time than the guys had and that ended up leaving me getting hurt. I also felt different with Dylan than I did with Greg. I didn't know how to break this down to something I could understand.

"Do you like him?"

"Yes."

"And we already know you've had sex with him. Which, I'm sorry to say that I still find hilarious in some ways, Aurora. Honestly, you really shocked me with that piece of information."

I frowned. "Why?"

"Oh, my dear, you aren't the spontaneous one, not in the slightest, so to find out you had a one-night stand nearly made me want to pee my pants. However, I think it's wonderful that you took control and loosened up a little, but we won't dwell on that."

I let out a sigh. This was my mother, not the

greatest advice giver there was. It was good to know she had a chuckle over my admittance.

"First, it's not weird."

"Really?"

My mother nodded. "Really, it's spontaneous. Some of the best lovers I've had were spontaneous."

She sounded exactly like Willow. Walker and I had heard her and many of her spontaneous lovers many nights through the walls from the confines of our bedroom. The next morning, the both of us shared in the embarrassment to see whatever flavour of the month had left the house.

"What if it's more than that, though?" I questioned.

"More than…spontaneous?"

"Yes."

"Are you asking me what to do if it's love?"

I shrugged, not entirely sure what it was I was asking. I thought back to the other night, in his apartment after all hell had broken loose in the club, how the sex that night had been different. It wasn't commanding like before, and there had been no laughter. Instead it was slow, passionate, and just… different. In the morning, we'd taken our time together, shared coffee and breakfast out on the balcony before we made our way into his shower before I'd left to go pick up Lorelai. Each time felt different, and I didn't know how to handle it.

"I don't know?"

"Well, only you can answer that, Aurora. I can't. You are the one who knows what you are asking."

I looked out over the water, at the sailors and their boats, my head full of questions that I didn't know how to answer. I bit my bottom lip as I thought about what it was I really wanted to ask my mother. Did I want to know what to do if it was love? Was I even ready for that? I took a sip of my coffee and cleared my throat.

"Maybe that is what I'm asking? Would you frown upon it if it was?"

"Heavens, Aurora. Why would I frown upon it? I think it's wonderful, and if you are right and it is love, then I say you should go for it. If being together makes the two of you happy, then nothing in the world should stop you."

"Not even the fact that you married his father?" I questioned, swallowing hard.

My mother sighed and sat back against the bench. "Aurora, you should know by now that what is here today for me could be gone in the blink of an eye tomorrow. It's why I never really get upset when it disappears. I take it for what it is, enjoy it while I have it, and if it disappears, then I pick up the pieces, brush them under the proverbial rug, and I move on. I've lived my entire life that way—after your father, that is."

Here she was telling me the exact thing I thought would have ended all my hurt by being spontaneous, and now here I was with a much bigger problem. Living my life and enjoying the moment had started this entire thing, and now here I was with feelings for Dylan, something that was never supposed to happen. However, I also was never supposed to see him again either.

"Seriously, Aurora, just live in the moment. Enjoy it and make the most of it. You'll regret it if you don't. Take things as they come."

Then my mother did something she hadn't done since I was a very little girl. She reached over and wrapped her arms around me, pulling me in for a hug.

"Thanks, Mom," I whispered.

"Now, I need to get going. I have lunch with Joe at the yacht club. Did you want to join us?"

I shook my head. "No, I have to get back home. Lorelai and I have a study group later this afternoon. Love you, and thanks, Mom."

"Anytime, my dear. See you soon."

I stayed on the bench and watched as my mother walked away. She seemed happy, happier than I'd seen her in a long time, and I really hoped that Joe was the one who'd be around for a while. He seemed to be good for her.

Chapter 13

Dylan

COACH DIDN'T LET up on practice today. Sweat poured from my head as I stepped off the ice. My legs were killing me, and I couldn't wait to get into the hot tub.

"Fuck, that was killer," Knox said, sitting down on the bench beside me breathing hard.

"Three more games, boys, three more…determines if we make the playoffs or not," Coach said as he stepped off the ice. "Don't fuck this up," he muttered, walking past us.

"What's gotten into him today?" Clay asked, sitting

down and squirting water into his mouth. "We haven't had a practice like that in ages."

"No idea," I muttered, squirting Gatorade into my mouth.

Coach returned and looked at us. "Oh, and when you guys are finished in the showers, meet me in the boardroom."

He looked directly at me as he told us to meet him. I swallowed hard. I'd had several meetings already this morning about what had happened Friday night at the club. I was in the clear, I already knew that, but the look on the coach's face made me worry another hammer was about to drop.

"Let's go, boys," I said, standing up.

The hot tub had never felt so good. I closed my eyes and sank into the water, listening to the guys banter back and forth. We didn't play tonight. Instead, we were heading off to our next away game in only a few hours.

"I'm going to see Stacy for a massage and some stretching," Knox said, climbing out of the hot tub.

"Don't forget coach wants to see us."

"He said to meet him after we're finished here. Besides, if I don't get this hamstring loosened, I'll be useless on the ice tomorrow night."

Knox had aggravated an old hamstring and hip injury three weeks ago and had been heading for treatment since. We couldn't afford to lose him now. "Alright, we'll meet you there," I said, climbing out of the hot tub and heading to the showers.

Forty-five minutes later, we all sat in the boardroom waiting for the coach to begin. I laughed at something Clay said when I caught sight of Pamela, one of our PR reps. She walked in and handed something to the coach, and then whispered something in his ear. He nodded, made a note, and then looked over at me. I swallowed hard. Something was going on.

My phone vibrated in my pocket, and I was about to reach for it when he stood up, making his way over to the door, which he closed. All the signs were there. Someone was in shit, and I knew damn well it was me.

"Alright, guys, listen, seems we have a minor problem on our hands, which has brought some bad press to the team."

Each of us looked at one another, wondering what could have caused that. Certainly, it couldn't have been the brief outbreak that had happened at the bar. No one had seen anything. At least I didn't think they had. My phone vibrated again in my pocket, so this time I pulled it out and looked at it.

There on my phone was the headline from Cam's Sports Desk. It said it all. As I read the words, I felt sick and lightheaded.

"So you've seen it," Coach said, looking directly at me.

The room was quiet as our eyes met.

"What is it?" Lucas questioned.

"Yeah, what is it?" Clay asked.

I swallowed hard and shoved my phone over toward them so they could see for themselves. The blood rushed from their faces, just like I'm sure it had done from mine.

"Pamela," the coach said, stepping to the side while she came to the front of the table.

"Hey, guys. I want to discuss what happened Friday night. It seems Dylan had a run-in with his ex-girlfriend Carlie at a local club on Friday. The same ex that caused all the trouble last year. The situation was taken care of immediately. However, she has now gone to the press."

The entire team turned and looked my way. I'd done everything I could for the better part of the year to keep myself out of the spotlight. I could only imagine what this news might do now. Hell, if she was malicious enough, it could end my contract with this team.

"Carlie is pregnant, and Dylan is about to be a happy father," Pamela announced as she read the beginning part of the article.

I shook my head as each one of the team turned

and looked my way. "Look, she is lying. You all know that. If she is pregnant, it's not mine. You all know I've been single for months, until just recently. If it's anyone's, it's Novak's."

Knox reached over and grabbed my phone from Clay's hand and opened the article, reading silently.

"Nope, not what it says here."

I glared at him, adrenaline coursing through my veins. I knew he was only doing it to get at me, maybe to break the tension, but I wasn't in the mood for his shit.

"It says here that it is yours," he said, tapping the screen on my phone.

"For fuck's sakes, man, you are with me everywhere I fucking go. When was the last time I was with her?"

"Knock it off, man," Clay growled at Knox. "Don't get him going."

Two guys on the team chuckled while a bunch of them started murmuring amongst themselves.

"Alright, that's enough!" Coach yelled, regaining control of the room again.

"I'll call my attorney and demand she provide a DNA test." I raised my voice loud enough that everyone could hear me over their murmurs.

"We are already on it," Pamela said, taking a moment to think. "Look, for the time being, no interviews—again. No one in this room is to say anything to anyone about this, anyone who's asked is to comment with no comment. The team's lawyers have already been contacted. They will make sure any videos that surface from Friday night are removed off social platforms, and they are working on a press release."

I felt sick.

CLAY, Lucas, Knox and I sat at a private table in the back of The Sushi Garden.

"There is also another problem at hand here, guys," Knox said, shoving a soft-shell crab roll into his mouth.

"What's that?" Clay asked.

I wanted this conversation to be over. Hell, I wanted this entire situation to be over. The worst thing I think I'd ever done was get involved with Carlie. She'd cost me enough over the last year, but it appeared she was back for more. She probably wouldn't be content until I'd lost everything.

"We're playing Novak's team tomorrow night."

That was all I needed to hear. I gripped my chopsticks hard enough that they should have broken.

"Whatever we do, we can't let our boy near him."

"Sort of impossible, don't you think?" Knox said, looking over at Clay. "They're both centers."

I closed my eyes and took a deep breath. If I made it through tomorrow night's game without a fight, it would be a miracle, I thought to myself. If I knew Novak, he probably put Carlie up to this little stunt just to get under my skin. We'd always hated one another, and it wasn't getting any better.

"It's fine. I'll be fine, guys."

"Isn't that what you said last time?" Knox asked.

"Yep, that was what he said," Clay added.

"Last time was different. The wound was raw, and besides, he asked for it," I said, getting my back up at the memory.

It happened right after I'd caught her with him. They were the second team we played that season. The wound was open and raw, and when we came face-to-face and he slurred those words at me, I saw nothing but red for the entire night.

"He may have, but that brief fight landed you in the sin bin for five minutes."

"It landed him in it for seventeen," I bit back.

"Look, why are we even rehashing this?" Clay asked, looking over at Knox and me.

"He's right, guys. This isn't the time," Lucas agreed. "We need to make sure that doesn't happen again. The playoffs are so close I can taste it. We can't lose that. We have a good chance of winning this year."

The way I was feeling, anything was possible at this point. I let out the breath I was holding and signalled for the bill.

I GLANCED down at my phone just as the limo pulled into the arena. I'd left a message for Aurora before leaving my apartment, and she was just now getting back to me.

Aurora: Hey sorry. Just got back from school, not sure I've caught you in time or not.

I SMILED as I read her message. After the shitty day I'd had, I'd never been so happy to hear from her.

Dylan: Still here. Just getting to the arena, heading out in about thirty.

Aurora: How long are you gone this time?

Dylan: Just two games, tomorrow and the next night. We'll be flying in after the game that evening.

Aurora: Good, can't wait to see you.

THAT MESSAGE COULD ONLY HAVE MEANT that she hadn't seen the news. At least I'd hoped she hadn't. I'm sure if she had, she'd have been inundating me with questions. This would give me the time I needed to tell her in my time without her jumping to conclusions. I planned to sit down with her the day I returned to let her know what was going on.

Dylan: See you then. I'll message you after the game tomorrow.

Aurora: Why not tonight?

Dylan: We'll be getting in late. I know you have to study.

Aurora: Yeah, but I can take a break.

Dylan: Okay, I'll message you once we land.

Aurora: I'll be looking forward to it.

I POCKETED my phone and climbed out of the limo and made my way to the changing room to grab my stuff.

"SORRY, school ran late today. I wanted to get back over to Vancouver to say good-bye before you left."

I closed my eyes. I'd wished we could see one another before we left as well, but because things had gone crazy at the arena after practice, it was probably better this way.

"Is everything okay?" she questioned. "You don't sound like yourself."

"Yeah, I guess I'm just tired. Practice was brutal," I lied.

I was worried about how Aurora may react when

and if she saw the news. Things had just seemed to sort themselves out after the night at the club. I didn't want this rumour to cause things to go sideways again.

"Maybe I should let you get some rest."

"No, I'm good."

"Can you hang on one minute. I have another call coming in. It could be Lorelai she's out with some girls."

"Sure thing."

I lay there as the phone went silent, waiting for her to come back. I placed my free hand behind my head and turned the TV on. I was about twenty minutes into a movie when Aurora finally returned.

"Sorry about that." She sniffled.

"What's wrong?" I asked immediately. I could hear she was upset.

"It's nothing…really."

"Aurora, come on, talk to me."

She went quiet, and then I heard her blow her nose. "Sorry, that was Greg."

Who the hell was Greg and why was he calling my girl. "Sorry?"

"Greg, my ex." She sniffled again.

Was she crying? I rolled over, giving her my undivided attention. "Aurora, what happened?"

"Nothing. It's stupid. Don't worry about me, I'm fine."

"No way. You're upset. What happened?"

"He's just an asshole. When he broke things off with me, he gave me zero reason. He apparently heard from Lorelai's ex, Hugo, that I'm dating again."

"So, what did he want?" I questioned.

Aurora was quiet for a few minutes.

"I'm afraid to tell you because I don't want you to think I'd ever—"

"Aurora, just tell me."

"He called me up to see if we'd be able to work things out and get back together."

"What was your answer?"

"No, of course."

"Okay, so if you said no, then why are you crying? You're obviously not going to tell me you're leaving me for him, so there should be no need to shed tears."

The line went quiet for a moment. Then she cleared her throat. "I don't think I could ever leave you."

I closed my eyes at her admission, wishing that I was with her at this moment. I wanted to see her face, to hold her close to me. This was the first time she'd really sort of told me how she was truly feeling about us, and I was miles and miles away from her.

"I wish I was with you right now."

"Same here." She sniffled.

Chapter 14

Aurora

I LET OUT a yawn as I shoved a pile of papers into the recycle bin. I'd stayed up until almost three talking with Dylan last night. It hadn't been the greatest idea when I had to be up early this morning for our last study group session.

"Are you sure you're up to cleaning and packing today? You look bloody exhausted." Lorelai asked, grabbing her books from the table and shoving them into her bag.

"Yeah, I promised. It needs to get done anyway. It won't be much longer before we have to find a new place back in Vancouver, so we might as well get a head start. The more stuff we can get packed, the better off we will be for a quick move-in date."

"Alright, well, how about we stop and grab something from Sip and Stir and then head back to the apartment and get started?"

"Good idea. I could use—" I broke into a yawn, and Lorelai let out a laugh.

"Yeah, I think you and lover boy there need to keep things to a normal hour."

I smiled and shook my head. "We didn't keep you awake, did we?" I questioned, feeling slightly embarrassed if we had.

"No, I'd of banged on the wall if you had of. I was out like a light once I got home."

After Greg interrupted things and Dylan talked me down, things turned a little heated. We'd even switched to video chat after so we could say good night to one another face-to-face. I'd feared that perhaps Lorelai heard things she shouldn't have.

"Sorry, we will try to have our calls earlier in the evening, okay."

"It's fine. Like I said, if I'd heard anything I'd have banged on the wall. Besides, their games go late, and I know how much Candace misses Phil while he is away. I wouldn't dare ask you not to make the most of the time you have."

Once we'd packed up our books, we grabbed food

and coffee and made our way back to the apartment. Feeling completely energized after having something to eat, we began cleaning. Lorelai tackled the living room and kitchen while I got the fun job of the washroom. I'd just rinsed down the tub and shower when I heard Lorelai call my name.

I dropped the sponge in the sink and ripped the rubber gloves off my hands.

"Hurry up…hurry up," Lorelai said as I opened the bathroom door and stepped out into the living room.

I glanced around. The room was still a disaster. She hadn't done a thing. I looked inside the two empty boxes we'd brought home to see she'd packed nothing up, either. I looked over at her to see she was sitting on the edge of the couch, her hands in the pouch of her sweater, watching TV.

"What is it? I thought you were cleaning and packing?" I asked, feeling annoyed.

"I was, but then I turned the TV on and look…" she said, pointing to the screen.

I turned and looked over my shoulder at the TV to see Dylan's face filling the screen. Shock filled me as I read the headline below. *Vancouver Dominator Dylan Hayes to be a father: ex-girlfriend pregnant.*

"Did you know about this?" Lorelai questioned.

I shook my head as I continued to listen to the

story. Now I really didn't know what to believe. She had been so convincing that perhaps this story was true and I really was the one being lied to.

"Well?"

I flopped down on the couch and sank into my usual spot and stared at the screen. They were showing clips from past games, and then they brought up a clip from last year. Dylan was fighting with some guy on the ice, and then it broke out to a picture of both him and Carlie walking away from some building.

"When we were on our date the other night, something happened at the club."

"Oh?"

"We were dancing. Knox, Clay, and Lucas had just arrived. Anyway, we were dancing, and then I was attacked by someone. I was ripped away from Dylan and thrown to the ground by my hair."

"What??? You mentioned nothing about this. Are you alright?"

"I am now. Yes. Or was. Anyway, it was her, the one in the picture. She said something about wanting him back and how they were planning on having a family."

"Oh god."

"Yeah, it was awful. Dylan was angry, and I just wanted away from it all."

"Wait a minute. So, then the butt dial…wasn't a

mistake," she said as I shook my head. "Why didn't you have me come get you?"

"I didn't feel a need to have you come get me. Part of me also wanted to hear him out."

"Well, I'm glad you did that. However, this is just crazy. Did he say anything to you?"

I shook my head.

"This woman sounds super desperate. It's like she is grasping at straws. I mean…wow."

I watched a little more and then looked at Lorelai. "She cheated on him with another Dominator. I can't remember his name…" I said, looking at the TV again to see the same clip of him fighting. "Wait…" I said, squinting to read the guy's jersey. "That's him."

"Novak?? She cheated on Dylan with that looser?" Lorelai asked.

I nodded. "That is what he said."

"God, my brother hated him. As did pretty much every guy on the team. He was just so full of himself."

We watched the clip again. I could clearly see Novak lean in and say something to Dylan, and that was when the fight began.

"I remember when that happened," Lorelai said, watching the screen with me. "He'd just been traded to the new team about a week prior."

Once again, the image flashed to Carlie and Dylan and their splitsville article and then to her statement about her current condition. She stood there speaking to a reporter, eyes full of tears as she broke down into fits of hysteria.

"So he said nothing to you about this? I mean, he must know about it now?" Lorelai asked.

"He said nothing to me at all," I muttered. "Just turn it off."

"Maybe he doesn't know yet?" Lorelai said, doing as I asked and shutting the TV off.

"You know as well as I do they have watchdogs everywhere. I mean, had you of seen how quickly the guys handled the other night, you'd of been shocked. They had PR called, lawyers called, and were even proceeding with using the restraining order that Dylan had put in place before we left the parking lot."

I knew Lorelai knew how fast they moved. Her brother had his share of bad publicity over the years, especially when he first came to the team.

"Well, if he knows, then why didn't he mention anything to you?" Lorelai questioned.

I shrugged. "I don't know. Maybe he doesn't know, and besides, the games tonight."

Just then the phone rang, and Lorelai grabbed it. I sat there looking at my phone on the table, wondering if he had messaged me and I'd just not seen it. I wasn't even sure I wanted to look.

"It's Candace. She got the invitations in for the

wedding and wants to know if we can come by after exams to help her stuff envelopes," Lorelai said.

I nodded. "Can you ask her something for me?" I whispered.

Lorelai nodded.

"Ask her if Phil ever keeps things from her?"

Lorelai frowned. "Hold on one second, Candace." She covered the mouthpiece and dropped it in her lap and looked at me. "What are you wanting to know?"

"Just ask her if Phil ever kept things from her regarding bad publicity?"

Lorelai shook her head but asked anyway. I could hear her answer, and then I heard her ask why?

"No, there has been nothing in the news about him. Aurora was just wondering is all. Yep, I'll let her know. Okay. See you then."

Lorelai hung up the phone and then turned to me. "Her words exactly. If he ever hid anything from me, he'd never use his man stick on me again."

I couldn't help but smirk from the expression on Lorelai's face as she repeated the words that her soon-to-be sister-in-law said.

"Excuse me, because after saying those words in relation to my brother- and sister-in-law, I think I'm going to have to wash my mouth out with soap now."

I couldn't help but giggle at the face she made as she got up and went into the kitchen, bringing us both back some Gatorade. While I sat there, I replayed our conversation earlier, how he seemed to not be bothered by anything. However, my problem had seemed to monopolize the conversation. Maybe he just hadn't wanted to upset me again, or perhaps Lorelai was right and he knew nothing about it.

"Here," she said, dropping my favourite blue Gatorade in my lap. "What are you thinking about?"

"Just about our conversation from last night. Lorelai, I really like him. and I'd hope he wouldn't hold something like this back from me after the events of the other night. I'd hope he'd be upfront and honest with me, especially if this is true and it is his baby."

"If it's bothering you so much, why don't you message him?"

I glanced at the time. It was a little after three. From what Dylan told me, they'd be just arriving at the arena by now. This was also an important game, and I wasn't sure I wanted to bring something like this up before it.

"I don't know."

"Okay, how about this? We'll finish cleaning, then we'll order in some pizza and wings, then we'll get ready and watch the game. You can text him while we wait for food if you still want to."

I thought about her suggestion and nodded.

"Okay."

Soon we were back into the swing of cleaning, and I'd forgotten about the news, at least as much as one could forget about the news after seeing someone accuse the man I liked. We each took a quick shower, and while Lorelai ordered pizza and wings, I got changed into my sweats. I was about to leave my room when I spotted Dylan's jersey in my closet and threw it on for good luck.

"Alright, get over here and sit down. Now are you ready to watch your first hockey game?" Lorelai questioned, dropping two cans of soda onto the coffee table, along with two plates.

I nodded. "I'll probably have a million questions."

"That's fine. Ask whatever you want," she said, looking up at me. "What the hell do you have on?" she questioned.

I looked down at myself, wondering if I had underwear stuck to my pants or something from the wash.

"The jersey? Where the hell did you get that?"

"Oh, Dylan gave it to me, didn't I tell you?"

"No, you didn't."

"When we went on our date, he gave it to me."

"Oh boy. You are done for."

I frowned and glanced at my phone and then looked back at Lorelai.

"Why?"

"Everyone knows you're his now." She winked.

I grabbed my phone again, looking to see if he'd messaged.

"If you want to message him, I'd do it now. Candace told me Phil said the guys were just about done getting ready. Maybe we should send him a pic of you in his jersey."

I shook my head. "No, I'll just wait to talk to him after the game."

It was then Lorelai got up off the couch and quickly turned, snapping a picture of me. She began furiously texting as I frowned.

"What are you doing?" I questioned.

"Sending it to my brother so he can forward it to Dylan." She giggled.

I got up and tried to rip her phone from her hand, but she bolted to the door just as the bell rang. Moments later, she returned with our food. The aroma of wings and pizza were enough to make my mouth water. I quickly opened the wings and took some, passing it to Lorelai, who took some as well.

I leaned back and took a bite of my pizza and watched as the guys skated out onto the ice. The camera immediately panned to Dylan. He skated around the rink, raising his stick in the air as fans cheered.

Lorelai let out a tiny laugh, and I looked over at her. "What?"

"Oh, nothing."

"No, what is it?"

"Look at you. I never in a million years thought I'd ever see that look on your face over a hockey player."

"What look?"

"This look…" Lorelai looked at the TV with a goofy look on her face, causing me to laugh.

"Shut up."

"I won't." She, too, began laughing.

The game started, and I watched as Dylan made his way to his position, just as the commentator brought up everything that was going on in the news.

"Can they hear that?" I questioned.

Lorelai shook her head, and I watched as a questioning look came over her face.

"What is it?" I asked.

"Oh, this isn't good."

"What?"

"The team they are playing. It's Novak's team. Maybe this isn't the game you should watch first."

The two players faced off. We both watched as the puck was dropped. Dylan got control of the puck and passed it over to Knox. Knox passed it back to Dylan just as Novak came in and body checked Dylan right into the boards.

"Don't tell me he's going after him again," Lorelai said under her breath.

Minutes later, Novak checked Dylan again, and then again for the third time. I could barely watch anymore as the next time he took a hit, he was down on the ice for a few minutes.

Halfway into the game, I'd had to run to the washroom, and when I came back the third period had just stared, the guys were losing 3 to 1, and I reached for another slice of pizza, taking my eyes off the screen for one second when Lorelai screamed.

"What? What is it?" I cried, adrenaline coursing through my veins. Dropping the slice of pizza back into the box, I looked up at the TV in time to see Dylan deliver a punch to Novak. The crowd went crazy as the two fought. Finally, they split, and one referee separated them, and that was when Novak went to punch, hitting the ref square in the face. Knox came in, pulling Dylan away.

"Oh this is bad," Lorelai muttered as we both watched as the commentators once again brought up the fight between the two players from a year and a half ago.

MY FIRST HOCKEY game turned out to be more exciting than I'd ever thought. Dylan had ended up in the sin bin, as Lorelai put it, more in this game than any other. The boys had lost, and Lorelai explained they had to win tonight if they were to go on to the finals. I almost felt like it was my fault they'd lost, even though I knew it wasn't.

I rolled over and stared at the clock. I figured I'd have heard from Dylan by now. It was after midnight. The game had ended over two hours ago, but my phone had remained silent. I placed my book on my side table and was just about to reach up and shut off my book light when my door opened.

"You still awake?"

"Yeah."

"Hear anything yet?" she asked, coming in and sitting on the end of my bed.

I'd always been thankful to have Lorelai in my life. She was always there when I needed her, but right now, all I wanted to do was talk to Dylan and find out exactly what had happened tonight and if he knew about the rumours that were running rampant.

"No," I said, letting out a sigh.

"I talked to Phil a few minutes ago. He said Dylan's pissed, so I'm sure he's probably just blowing off steam with the guys. Don't sweat it, he'll message tomorrow."

"Is your brother out with everyone?"

"No, he always goes back to his room and calls Candace."

"That's nice of him. Well, thanks for the update, I guess. Sleep well," I said, my voice clearly reflecting my disappointment.

Lorelai got up and went to leave my room, when I stopped her.

"So, you seemed to get along with Knox well the other night."

She shook her head. "Don't even start. I knew him once, a long time ago, and let me tell you, I'd never go down that path."

I couldn't help but laugh as she continued shaking her head as she made her way to my bedroom door.

"You say that about everyone that you date or could be a potential date." I giggled.

"Well, that's because some truly deserve it, and I never dated him, nor would I, so that statement is no longer true." She giggled. "Sleep well. Oh, Aurora, do me a favour and never mention that man's name to me again." She giggled.

Chapter 15

Dylan

EVERYONE WAS silent as we finished dinner. Penelope sat across from my father and Aurora sat across from me. I looked up to see her drag her fork around her plate, shoving at the remains of her dinner. She lifted her eyes and met mine, giving me a soft smile.

The silence in the room was unbearable, and the tension could be cut with a knife. My father cleared his throat and immediately Aurora looked back down at her plate.

"Aurora, why don't you help your mother clean up? I want to talk with Dylan alone," he said, placing his empty wineglass down on the table with a little more force than I expected.

"Joe, she doesn't need to help, it's fine," Penelope said, grabbing my plate and placing it on top of hers.

"She does," Joe barked before getting up from his chair and looking over at me. "She'll do as she is told to do in this house."

Aurora met my eyes and winced, then, with shaking hands, she reached over for my father's plate, while the tension in the room continued to grow.

"Let's go," my father barked at me and headed down the hall toward his office.

I was expecting this mood from my father. What I wasn't expecting was to find Aurora here for dinner. My father had called me just after I'd called Aurora last night. I'd just finished explaining everything to her about what she'd seen on the news and was relieved to find out that she was going to stand by my side. We'd said good night, and I'd just pulled out of the parking lot, when my phone rang again. My father wasn't so understanding. He barked at me the entire drive home and then demanded I show up today. He'd put me in an unbelievably bad mood, not to mention confrontational, which had carried over into today.

"What?" I barked as I walked into his office and slammed the door shut.

"Sit the fuck down and don't slam doors in this

house."

I leaned against the back of the chair on the opposite side of my father's desk. I wasn't putting up with this shit today. My father turned around and looked at me.

"I told you to sit down," he barked again.

"No," I said, crossing my arms over my chest and squaring off to him. "Oh, and as for the door slamming, I learned from the best."

"Alright then, big man, what the fuck do you think you're doing?"

"About?"

"The shit that is all over the news?"

"I've got my lawyers on it, as well as the team's lawyers."

"Is it true? Did you knock her up?" he questioned, crossing his arms in front of his chest as well.

"No."

My father sort of chuckled at my answer and shook his head.

"What?"

"Have your lawyers gotten back to you with the answers about the paternity test that they were talking about on the news?"

"No. Not yet."

"You are absolutely certain you didn't knock her up?"

I rolled my eyes and met my father's eyes. He'd been this way when we'd broken up. Giving me shit about ending a relationship that he was certain was the best thing in my life.

"Yes."

"Then what the fuck were you thinking during the game?"

"What?"

"The fight, Dylan. What the fuck were you thinking, throwing the game by getting into a fight?"

"First, I didn't throw the game. In fact, I didn't throw the game at all. We fucking lost."

"Because your mind was elsewhere. I can always tell when your mind is elsewhere because you play like shit."

"Give it a rest, Dad. I don't need to hear this right now."

"It's true."

"Yeah, sure, and I've already heard it from the coach. You think I need to hear it from you, too?"

"Damn right you do. Fuck, Dylan, I sunk thousands of dollars into you, fucking thousands. I didn't do it so you could fuck up your career."

"How did I fuck up my career?"

"You don't get it, do you? Until we have a fucking answer from this test, people are going to consider it to be true, and so am I."

"Believe what you want. You always have, but know this, I haven't been with Carlie since last year. I've had restraining orders on her. I've sent her cease and desist notices after she dragged me through the mud after our breakup that she caused. She cost me thousands of dollars. Why do you think I'd ever get involved with that again?"

"Because I know how men are. I am one. We do stupid things, which brings me to the next matter I want to discuss with you."

I turned away from my father for a moment. I didn't want to hear any more. He never believed a word I said. I didn't know why I'd thought this time would be any different.

"Did you hear me?"

I closed my eyes for a moment, taking a deep breath. He was pushing my buttons, every single one of them, and I wasn't sure how much more I could take. It was like the other night on the ice with Novak. He pushed me until I blew, and my father was going to do the same.

"Sit down," he barked.

"I'm fine. I'll stand."

My father walked over to the window and looked out onto the backyard. He was silent for a moment, then he pulled out a cigar from his humidor, cut the end, and lit it. He stood there puffing away on it, then cleared his throat.

"Penelope told me something disturbing the other day."

I straightened up to my full six-foot height and crossed my arms, towering over my father by a few inches. "Okay."

"She said you and Aurora have been fooling around together."

"We aren't…I mean…we are, but it's not what you think."

"Not what I think? Dylan, I wasn't born yesterday. This is beyond disturbing."

"First, we aren't fooling around."

My father shook his head and smirked. "Really? What would you call it?"

"Dad, I like her a lot. We aren't just fooling around."

"Dylan, do you have any idea how disturbing this is? You guys are basically brother and sister."

"I take it Penelope didn't tell you how we met?" I said, glaring at my father.

"No, and frankly, I don't give a damn how you met."

I clenched my fists and locked my jaw. He always thought he had power over people, and that was one thing I hated about him more than anything.

"Dad, we met way before…"

"What part of I don't want to hear it don't you get? I want you to end things with her immediately."

"Would you listen to me?" I said through clenched teeth.

"Dylan, I'm done listening. You're nothing but an immense disappointment. I'm giving you until the weekend to end things with Aurora, otherwise I'll end it for you."

I clenched my hands into fists and glared at my father. I wasn't putting up with this. He never listened to anyone but himself. He squared off with me, waiting to see what I'd do. I wanted to hit him, but then remembered Aurora and her mother were in the kitchen. Instead of taking out my anger, I turned and walked out. He followed right behind me, shouting at me the entire way. Instead of saying anything to anyone else, I stormed right out the front door, slamming it behind me. I was just about to my car when I heard Aurora call after me. I couldn't talk to her right now. I was too fucking angry, so, pretending not to hear her, I climbed into my car and slammed the door shut and raced out of the driveway.

I'D STOPPED by Knox's place and we'd completed our workout for today. That had enabled me to work off my anger and frustration in a better way than heading home and getting drunk would have.

I pulled my shirt off over my head and dropped it on the table, then adjusted the pillow behind my head and went back to reading when I heard a light knock on the door. I glanced at my watch. It was well after eleven. I placed my book down, wondering who it could be. If it was my father, I was almost certain there'd be a fight. Another soft knock had me heading to the door. Pulling it open, it surprised me to see Aurora standing there, her eyes red from crying. She said nothing; she stepped inside and crashed into me, wrapping her arms around me.

I pulled her inside, shut the door, and wrapped my arms around her.

"What's going on?" I questioned when she finally stopped crying.

"Your dad kicked me out of the house."

"What?" Anger coursed through my veins. I hated the man more now than ever.

"He came storming into the kitchen and told Penelope I had to leave. They started fighting…and he whispered something to my mom about me, which made her burst into tears. I didn't stay around to wait and find out what he said, but by the time I got to the door, they were fighting. I grabbed my stuff and left. My mom chased after me, but he grabbed her and pulled her back into the house and wouldn't let her go."

"He told me that your mom told him about us. He demanded I break it off with you. When I refused, he gave me an ultimatum. He said either I ended things or he would. That's why I left."

"Why would he say that?"

"He's pissed with me over the news and the game, and he's always thought he can control everything. Just ignore it. It will blow over," I said, pulled her against me. "Now, why aren't you at home? It's late." I pulled her inside and over to the couch where we sat down.

"I didn't want to go home. I wanted to see you. You left in such a hurry and said nothing to anyone. When I left, I drove all the way to the ferry and pulled over on the side of the road. I sat there crying for a while, debating whether to go home to study or come here. Then Lorelai called, panicking about the exam and worried about our job applications. She wouldn't let me get a word in edgewise, and that was when I knew I couldn't go home and face her. I was too upset, so I came here."

She lifted her eyes and met mine, her bottom lip trembling. I wanted to make everything go away for both of us. I leaned down and took her mouth with mine in a slow and gentle kiss. As we parted, she opened her eyes.

"I'm glad you came here," I whispered. "I needed you."

I flipped the light switch to the off position, took her hand, and pulled her down the hall to the bedroom.

WE LAY WRAPPED in one another's arms the next morning. I pressed a kiss to the side of her neck and she let out a soft moan.

"Morning beautiful," I whispered.

"Morning," she whispered, giggling as I playfully gripped her side, tickling her.

She shifted positions and wrapped her arm around me, kissing me.

When our lips parted, I looked down into her face. Those gorgeous green eyes of hers stared back at me in question.

"What's on your mind?" I questioned.

"It's nothing."

"It's something, I can tell," I said, rubbing the tip of her nose with mine.

"Are you going to let your father have his way regarding us?"

I looked into her eyes and brought my hand to her cheek, then brought my lips to hers. "Not a fucking chance."

"What if he forces it?"

"Let him try. There isn't much one can do to force two people apart when it comes to love."

Her eyes flew to mine, shock lining them. The word had slipped from my mouth. Not that I doubted what it was I was feeling, it was more that I wasn't sure she was ready to hear it.

"Are you saying that you're…um…in love…"

I brought my forefinger to her lips and looked into her eyes.

"I think I'm falling for you," I whispered. "Actually, I'm pretty damn sure I have."

The look in her eyes was nothing but shock. I was afraid that I may have blown this entire thing with her with that admission.

"You don't need to say anything back. It slipped," I said quietly.

She looked up at me, then put her hand behind my head and brought her lips to mine. When we parted, she said nothing. She just snuggled up closer to me and closed her eyes while I held her in my arms.

"I think I'm falling too," she whispered.

Chapter 16

Aurora - One Week Later

I WALKED down the university's steps and out into the fresh summer air. I took a seat on the stairs and waited for Lorelai, who was inside speaking with another student. It was our last day; we were finally free, having just written our last exam.

I pulled my phone from my pocket to see a message from Dylan congratulating us on our last day. I was about to reply when the doors opened, and I heard Lorelai behind me.

"Thank god!"

I couldn't help but laugh as she sat down beside

me, looking lighter than I'd seen her in the past few years. She also looked completely exhausted.

"Oh, I forgot to tell you I heard from the condo board. We can go by tonight if you want and see the place in Vancouver," Lorelai said, opening the email she'd received and sharing it with me.

I had mentioned nothing to Lorelai yet, but Dylan had already asked me to move in with him now that we were out of school. Since I wasn't sure of the answer myself, I knew if I moved in with him, I'd have to tell Lorelai before she signed the agreement. She wouldn't be able to afford the place on her own, especially if we didn't get the job with the Dominators, which we were still waiting to hear from.

"Sure, I guess we can go check it out."

"Is something wrong?" she questioned. "Did you want to look for something else? This one is higher priced."

I shook my head. "No, the place is fine. Guess I'm just tired. I was up late getting some study time in." I half smiled, knowing the truth was I was on the phone with Dylan for half the night when I should have been studying.

"Well, why don't we blow this place? We've spent enough time here."

"Funny you say that. I think I'm going to miss it, in some messed-up way." I giggled.

"Me too, and in some I won't."

We both laughed and then headed to the car.

I CAREFULLY PLACED the salmon onto the baking sheet and seasoned it perfectly, then slid it into the oven while Lorelai made the salad. The doorbell rang, and I ran to answer it only to find a box sitting on the porch wrapped with a red ribbon.

"Who is it?" I heard Lorelai ask.

"A box," I muttered, locking the door back up and heading into the kitchen with it.

"Sorry, who was it?" she asked again, tossing the salad.

"What?" I questioned.

"I asked you who was at the door."

"It's a box." I shrugged, pulling at the red ribbon and lifting the lid to see a bottle of wine and a card.

Lorelai made her way over and pulled the wine from the box. "Oh, it's an expensive one. Candace and Phil are having this at their wedding. Who's it from?" she questioned, reading the label.

I opened the card to see 'Congratulations' written

on the front of it, and on the back, 'Hope you enjoy. Sorry I can't be there. Love Dylan.'

"It's from Dylan," I answered, placing the card on the table, which Lorelai picked up right away.

"Ahhh, how sweet! He can't be here, but he's still thinking of you." She swooned, gesturing to the cupboard for two glasses.

Dylan had plans with the guys from the team tonight, but he'd promised he'd be here in spirit.

I handed her the corkscrew and grabbed the two glasses, placing them on the table while I quickly checked the fish. Lorelai had just poured the wine and passed me one glass when the phone rang.

"Ugh, don't drink just yet. We need to cheers each other," she said, reaching for the phone.

I watched as she listened to whatever was being said. She nodded, mumbled a few things, and then agreed we'd see whoever it was on Monday. I frowned as she hung up, wondering who it was. When she said nothing, I placed my wineglass down and placed my hands on my hips.

"Well, you going to tell me what that was about?" I questioned.

She looked at me and nodded.

"Okay then, tell me, what are we doing on Monday?"

Lorelai giggled and then jumped up and down.

"That was the head of the sports therapy department with the Dominators. We are both to report to our place of employment Monday morning to go over our schedules."

"What?" I questioned, not sure I totally believed her. "Are you serious?"

"Completely."

"Oh, my god!" I screamed, joining her in her celebratory jumping as we both laughed and hugged.

"Okay, let's cheers!" I screamed.

We both grabbed our glasses and congratulated each other and then we both took a sip. I closed my eyes as I took a drink. It had to be the best wine I'd ever tasted.

"Dylan has good taste," Lorelai said, winking at me.

"Of course he does." I giggled. "He's dating me."

We both laughed and took another drink.

"Are things getting serious between the two of you?"

I'd just put my fork down when my cell phone vibrated on the table. I glanced at the screen and frowned when I saw my mother's name there with a message to call her.

"What is it?" Lorelai asked.

I got up without answering her and grabbed my phone, dialing quickly.

"Aurora, what is it?" Lorelai asked again, panic setting on her face.

"It's my mom," I whispered, just as she picked up the phone. "Mom, I was going to call you right after dinner," I said into the phone. "I've got great news."

My mother said nothing. Instead, I heard her sniffle. Was she crying?

"Mom? What's wrong?" I questioned.

The line was silent for a long while before I heard her sniffle again. "Aurora, can I come and stay with you and Lorelai for a bit?"

I frowned, glancing around our small two-bedroom apartment that we'd be leaving in a couple of weeks if all went well. "What is going on?" I asked.

"God, Aurora, I feel like such a fool. Joe, he isn't the man I thought he was."

"What? Mom, what are you talking about?"

"Please, Aurora, I have nowhere to go. I'm at the ferry terminal in Victoria. I need you to come get me."

MOM and I sat on the couch in the living room while Lorelai made some tea.

"What happened?" I questioned as I placed a cool

cloth on the back of her neck to help her calm down. When I'd found her, she was in tears, and she cried the entire way to the house, not saying so much as one word to me.

"I'm leaving him. He's a horrible man," she said, crying once again.

I couldn't remember my mother being this upset over a breakup before. She used to just pick up the pieces and head to the local pub, have a delightful party by herself or with someone else to get it out of her system, and then continue with life. I didn't understand what the difference was this time.

"What happened?"

"Remember when he whispered something to me after Dylan stormed out of the house?"

I nodded, watching as Lorelai placed a tray on the coffee table along with a plate of peanut butter chocolate chip cookies.

"I didn't want to tell you what it was he said, but you knew I was upset."

"Upset? Mom, I've never seen you brought to tears so fast."

"He told me that my whore of a daughter had better never set foot in the house again."

My stomach sank. Had I caused their breakup?

"Why would he say that?"

"Because I was stupid, and I told him about you and Dylan."

I glanced at Lorelai, who shrugged her shoulders.

"Mom, it's fine. You did nothing wrong. Dylan knows he knows. He says he doesn't care what his father says."

"He should. He told me he would force Dylan to break things off with you. If he didn't do as he wanted, then he would put an end to it. After you left, he told me to tell you not to bother coming back to the house until I made sure you understood you weren't to have any more relations with Dylan.

She blew her nose into the tissues she was holding and looked at me with red, puffy eyes. I passed her the box to take a few more tissues so she could wipe the tears that had fallen again.

"Mom…" I said, patting her shoulder, trying to comfort her.

"It's okay, Aurora. I'll be fine," she said, straightening her back and sitting up taller. "What I won't have happen is someone to tear about two people who are clearly in love."

"Mom, you don't have to do that."

My mom blew her nose again, wiped the tears, and then met my eyes. She took hold of my hand and softly smiled for the first time since I'd picked her up. "Aurora, I've never been that good of a mother to either you or Walker, but that doesn't mean I can't start now."

"Mom, you have. We never went without."

"That is true, but you went without me. I was absent most of your life. I mean, you'd rather call me Penelope than Mom. That is saying something."

"I call you that because that is what you said you preferred."

"Well, okay, fine, that is true. However, this is what I'd prefer. I'm going to sacrifice this relationship for you. I'm leaving Joe. You deserve to have the best, and I've never seen you so confused over someone before that you'd actually ask me for advice. So, if it's okay, I'll stay here for a few days until I can get my things from Joe's and find a place of my own. I'll get looking right away."

I looked at Lorelai, not sure what to think. Like me, she looked just as confused, and she just shrugged again. I'd thought everything was fine between my mother and Joe, and I'd never have thought she'd give up something like that for me.

"Sure, Mom. I'll grab some blankets, and we will pull out the hideaway bed."

She picked up her tea and took a sip, then took a bite of a chocolate chip cookie and sat back on the couch.

"IT'S like the twilight zone, Walker. Mom is a mess."

My brother had called twenty minutes ago in a panic after receiving a call from Mom. She'd shut her phone off after I'd talked to her in case Joe was trying to call. When Walker couldn't get through, he called me.

"I know. She sounded gutted on the phone. What happened?"

"Mom said she is leaving Joe," I whispered into the mouthpiece, hoping that by now she was asleep. I didn't want her to overhear my conversation and get all upset again.

"Why?"

"I guess she told Joe about Dylan and I. Joe got angry, said I was a whore and wasn't welcome at the house any longer until we'd broken it off."

"I see," Walker replied.

"Mom said she feels bad that she was absent most of my life. That I'd rather call her Penelope than Mom, and I guess she wants to change that. She said she wants to make up for being absent most of our lives, and the way to do that is for her to sacrifice so that Dylan and I can be together. So, she is giving up her relationship with him for me." I sighed, still feeling horrible that she'd felt it necessary to give up on a relationship that was good for her.

"Well, Aurora, you can't stop her. I mean, maybe on the outside we think it was good for her, but perhaps there were things we didn't see."

Leave it to my brother to be the voice of reason when I'd rather mentally kick myself for causing her unhappiness.

"What do you mean?"

"Maybe Joe isn't all that he's cracked up to be. I mean, most of the time I was there, I felt like he was putting on a show. There was just something about him I didn't like. He was almost too kind, too accommodating for my liking."

I thought back to what he was saying and could see where he was coming from. It was true. He was too nice, too accommodating, especially with us and my mother. Well, he wasn't so nice to Dylan the other night though. I'd heard him yelling from the office.

"Maybe you're right. Maybe this is the reason Mom has been waiting for."

"I think so. Don't be too hard on yourself, but whatever you do, be careful with Dylan."

"Why?"

"Just be careful. I don't want to find you in a similar situation."

I appreciated my brother's concern for me, but Dylan was nothing like his father. In fact, he was the complete opposite. I didn't want to dismiss his concerns, though.

"I will, I promise. You'd be the first to know if something wasn't right. I promise you."

"You better. Well, I have to go. My time is up. Tell Mom to call me once she is feeling up to it. Love you both."

"Love you too."

Chapter 17

Dylan

KNOX, Clay, Lucas, and I sat in the boardroom looking over our new contracts. It had been a relief when Clay called and said he was bringing them over this morning after the gym. I'd been worried about my position with the Dominators, especially after everything that went down with Carlie, and I knew Knox was worried about his re-aggravated injury.

"Looks pretty standard," Knox said, shoving his copy back into the manilla envelope. "Guess I'll have my lawyer look it over to make sure everything is line."

"Same here," I muttered, shoving mine back into the envelope too."

Clay and Lucas did the same before sitting back in the chair, relaxing a bit.

"Told you that you had nothing to worry about," I said to Knox.

"Ah, you never know. I could be considered a weak link."

"Fuck them if they think that. You're a fucking awesome player, better than most," I said, tapping the envelope.

"Have you heard anything about Carlie yet?"

I shook my head just as my phone vibrated against the table. I glanced at the screen, wondering if it was Aurora, but it was my lawyer.

"Finally. I'll be right back," I muttered, grabbing my phone and heading to the hall for some privacy.

"Hello."

"Dylan, it's Thomas."

I'd been waiting on pins and needles for his call for days and I hoped he had the answers I wanted to hear.

"Hey, Thomas, any news?" I questioned.

"Good news. Between me and my partner and the lawyers with the Dominators, we have been able to get in touch with Carlie and her lawyers. We could get them to agree to her taking a paternity test."

"Perfect," I said, breathing a sigh of relief.

"We should have the results in a couple of days."

I closed my eyes and silently thanked the man

upstairs. "I'm not worried about anything, Thomas. I wouldn't go to all this trouble if it were true."

"I know that."

"While I have you on the phone, I just got my new contract. I'd like another set of eyes on it if that is okay. My agent has already looked it over, but I just want to be on the safe side."

"No problem. Send it over as soon as you can."

"Okay, Thomas, and thanks for the update. I've got to run, but I'll tell you I cannot wait for this to be all behind me."

"No doubt. Talk soon."

I'd just pocketed my phone and was about to head back into the boardroom when I felt it vibrate again. Pulling it from my pocket, I answered it immediately.

"Hello!"

"Dylan, it's your mother. How are you doing, darling?"

My mother had been living in Italy for the better part of the year, and it was rare I ever heard from her. She probably heard the gossip about me and wanted to know if it was true. That was usually the only time she ever called.

"Hey, Mom. How's Italy?"

"Wonderful. You really should plan to come over soon and see me. You are on a break now."

I closed my eyes and pinched the bridge of my

nose. I hadn't seen my mother since my parents separated ten years ago. She'd packed up, moved on, and left me with my father. We kept in touch through text messages, the occasional phone call, and sometimes an email. Aside from that, our relationship was pretty much non-existent. The last time I'd heard from her had been when things went crazy with Carlie and I was all over the news. The time before that was over three years ago when my father broke it off with his last girlfriend.

"I'll have to see, Mom. We just got our new contracts today."

"Does that mean you won't get vacation time?"

I hated to break it to her, but I wasn't all that keen on going to see her. She was practically a stranger, and with everything that had gone on over the last few weeks, I needed a break, not a vacation. Plus, with the contracts coming out, it meant that practices could start early, and I wanted to make sure I got to spend as much time with Aurora as I could before the season started.

"Let me guess, Dylan, you're too busy to see your mother. That's fine, I understand. Now, what is this I heard about your father? His latest marriage has fallen through the cracks."

I almost choked on the water I'd gotten from the vending machine a few moments ago. She lived on the other side of the world, with zero communication with either of us, and yet she knew things.

"Where did you hear that?" I questioned.

"Minga, your father's neighbour. She called right away when she saw, oh goodness, I forget whatever her name is, run out on him."

"Penelope, and that can't be true. They are very much in love," I replied.

When I'd left the other night, my father was in a mood. He was angry at me. I knew he had a temper, but I doubted he'd ruin a good relationship due to me.

"That might be what you think, Dylan, but let me tell you this. Your father is a completely different man on the relationship side of things. He has a very cruel side to him, and he never stops to think about what he might do to the other person. Perhaps she saw what was in front of her and decided she didn't want that anymore."

"Mom, I'm sure I don't know."

I didn't want to believe what it was she was saying about him. I knew he wasn't always the best he could be. I mean, look how angry he was over the newscast about me. He spewed at me like he didn't believe me. I knew how my father could be toward me, but I really didn't want to think that he could be that way to a woman, so much so that she wouldn't want to be with him. Plus, I really liked Penelope and had hoped that maybe this one would be it.

"Dylan, it would be so nice to see you. I miss my son."

She may miss me, but she certainly had not tried to communicate. "Well, Mom, I'll see what I can do and try to make it over there. I'll let you know."

"That would be wonderful. We could visit the sites and I could show you some of my favourite places. It would be nice to get to know my son again."

Even though she couldn't see me, I nodded.

"That sounds great, Mom. I have to run. I'm going to be late for a meeting."

"Go get them, sweetie. Remember, I love you."

"Love you too."

I hung up the phone and walked back into the boardroom to find the guys talking about the past season and where we'd gone wrong. I sat down, feeling relieved that I'd heard from Thomas and that things finally seemed to be coming to a close.

"Everything good?" Knox asked quietly.

"Everything is great," I said.

Chapter 18

Aurora

LORELAI and I waited for the elevator up to Dylan's condo. I went to step inside as the door opened, only to come face to chest with Dylan as he stepped out.

"Hey, baby," he said, placing a kiss on my cheek as he wrapped his arms around me in a protective embrace.

We were going to look at the condo tonight, and we asked Dylan if he would mind coming to look at it with us. Neither of us felt confident enough to decide without someone who'd been through this before. He told me he'd be happy to do it.

"Lorelai, how are things?" Dylan asked.

"Good. Thanks for doing this, Dylan."

"Not a problem. I was happy when Aurora called. I was hoping to get to see her after the contract meeting."

"How did that go? You mentioned nothing."

"Signed again. Can't get rid of me that easy." He chuckled, pressing a kiss to my lips.

"That's great," Lorelai replied. "Congratulations."

"Did your brother hear anything yet?" I questioned, knowing that she'd been worried when I told her Dylan had.

"Not sure. I talked to Candace earlier, but she said nothing. I know they were nervous about this year."

"Don't worry, he'll get signed. They took Knox back." Dylan winked.

"What's about me?" a voice asked behind us.

Lorelai and I turned to see Knox step out of the elevator, curiosity on his face.

"Not a thing," I said as Dylan chuckled.

"You girls ready?" Dylan asked.

"Yep. Let's go."

"Wait. Here are some waters," Knox said, handing a water bottle to each of us.

"Wait, he's coming?" Lorelai questioned, looking at me as I shrugged..

"Yes, he was here when you girls called. I figured we'd bring him along for a second set of eyes and then we'd go to see a movie or out for dinner," Dylan said.

"Sounds great." I said looking over at Lorelai who had a funny look on her face.

"Something wrong?" Dylan questioned.

"Aurora, can I see you for a moment?" Lorelai asked.

"Give us a minute," I said, turning to Dylan.

He nodded, and they both waited while Lorelai and I stepped outside.

The moment the door closed, and the guys were out of earshot, Lorelai turned to me.

"Aurora, I'm not sure that we need both of them to go."

"Well, I'm certainly not going to tell him he has to stay here. I know you aren't a fan of his, but it's only a few hours, and another set of eyes hurt nothing. Besides, he may grow on you."

"I doubt that."

"I don't understand what your issue is with him. He seems super nice. Give the guy a chance."

Lorelai shook her head and crossed her arms. "We have to get going or we'll be late," she said, heading toward my car.

"I think we are taking Dylan's car. Hold up."

"We're all going together?" She frowned.

"It makes the most sense." I shrugged.

I signaled to the guys to hurry, and together the four of us walked across the parking lot to Dylan's car.

DYLAN and I walked hand-in-hand through the condo, talking amongst ourselves as Lorelai and Knox walked behind us.

"I want to check out the bedrooms. We should decide now which ones we like. That way we won't fight over it on moving day." I giggled.

"We don't fight." Lorelai laughed.

"We will if we both end up wanting the same room."

We'd looked at all three bedrooms, and when I walked into the last one, I knew I wanted it. It was a pale purple, which was my favorite color. It had a gorgeous view of the city and a partial view of the water. "I think I'll take this one," I said.

"I figured, it's your favorite color."

"Which one are you going to take?" Knox questioned, turning to Lorelai.

"Not sure."

"I think you should take the one at the end of the hall. A complete view of the water."

Lorelai glanced at me. "I think I'll take the other one."

"Why on earth would you do that?" Knox asked. "I could tell the second you walked into that room you loved it."

"How do you figure?" she said, crossing her arms in front of her. "You don't know me."

"If you'd have seen your face looking out those windows, you'd know you loved it."

Lorelai crossed her arms in front of her and shook her head. "That room will be cold as hell in the winter, and I hate being cold."

I looked at Dylan, then at Lorelai. I'd known her forever, and the one thing I knew about her was she was always warm. It wasn't unusual for her to be in shorts and a T-shirt the entire winter while I was freezing.

"Lorelai, that isn't true," I said, rolling my eyes.

She lifted her eyes to mine. "It is. I hate being cold."

"Okay, but you have to admit it has the nicer of the two ensuites," Knox said, coming out from the one adjoining my room. "It has a huge soaker tub too, which would be perfect after work all day."

"I shower," she gritted. "Who the hell wants to sit in a tub of their own filth?"

I couldn't believe what I was hearing. Lorelai had

always loved taking baths. She was what I called the bathroom hog. Once she got in that tub in our apartment, she was in there for a good hour, normally lost in her book.

"What has gotten into you?" I questioned, pulling her out into the hall.

"In a bit of a bad mood, I guess."

"Okay, so then you want the bedroom with no bathroom and barely any windows?"

She gave me a funny look and nodded. That was when Knox stepped out into the hallway and put his arm around her. Her body stiffened. Dylan and I could barely contain our laughter as we looked at them.

"You need to loosen up a bit there," Knox said, tweaking her chin.

She closed her eyes. I could tell she was fuming as she stepped away from him. "Aurora, can we please check out the kitchen and living room again?"

She walked down the hall, leaving the three of us behind. I looked at both Dylan and Knox. "Sorry, guys, I don't know what has gotten into her today."

"PMS," Knox said.

I couldn't help but giggle, but I knew if Lorelai had heard that she'd have come back to us and probably beat poor Knox to death.

LORELAI AND KNOX had been at each other the entire time we'd been checking out the condo. It had gotten so bad at one point that I'd pulled her into another room while Dylan and Knox looked over the contract. Everything the poor guy had said she'd fought against.

We'd been planning on having dinner together after checking out the condo, but Dylan and I agreed we'd do dinner tomorrow after our rock-climbing adventure. There was no way we could have taken the pair of them out together, fighting the way they were. So once we were back at the condo, we said good-bye, parted ways, and Lorelai and I headed over to Sip and Stir.

I sat in our usual booth, while Lorelai picked up our order. She'd calmed down considerably after we'd left and was now looking a little tired. She smiled at me as she carried over the tray filled with two coffees, two sandwiches, and two donuts, and placed it in the centre of the table.

"You're sure you are comfortable signing the lease? I know two weeks wasn't much time to organize moving, but you must admit this is exciting! Plus, we will be closer to work."

"It's signed. There is no going back now," I replied, reaching for my sandwich. I wasn't sure I wanted to talk about the condo right this moment. The entire events of the afternoon had put me into a mood.

"Look, I'm sorry about this afternoon," she muttered, dumping three packets of sugar into her coffee.

"What got into you? That's what I'd like to know."

"Ugh, he is just so frustrating."

I giggled. "Lorelai, he did nothing. It was all you. Everything he suggested or said, you jumped on him."

"I didn't."

"You did! Goodness, when he suggested we paint the living room in a nice earth tone color instead of the horrendous yellow, you immediately ripped his head off, and you hate yellow."

"I never did."

"Please! Give it a rest! I also couldn't believe you said you wanted the other bedroom. That gorgeous bedroom was the reason you even wanted to check that condo out. I know you were doing it to just to be argumentative."

Lorelai let out a sigh and dropped her sandwich to her plate, putting her face into her hands.

"I couldn't help it. He just makes me angry."

"How? The man literally did nothing! So either you're really hung up on him, or you hate his guts for something you haven't told me about. So, you best spill it."

I knew Lorelai hadn't had the best dating history. I also knew that the break with Hugo nearly ruined her, especially after she slept with my brother to get over him. She'd been single ever since. She'd already told me that the next guy she dated would have to be a good guy, not one that would rake her through the coals again. I'd actually never seen her act this way before with anyone, so I was guessing there had to be a story hidden here somewhere.

"Fine, you win, you are right. Knox and my brother were the best of friends. Growing up, I'd always crushed on him, but there was always such a huge age bracket between us, he'd never give me the time of day. When he finally found out about my crush on him, he did nothing but tease me about it."

"Well, now that you are older, perhaps he finds you attractive. Maybe he likes you now. However, with the attitude you just gave him, I can't see that being true for very long," I said, more to bug her than anything.

"Don't you dare say that." she said, giving me a disgusted look.

"Why not? I hate to break it to you, but he is hot, and he seems super sweet, and so what if he used to tease you? I'm sorry, but that doesn't give you the right to treat him the way you are."

Lorelai shook her head. "He isn't hot, and he deserves it. He's just like all the rest."

"So you're angry with him because he used to bug you? What is wrong with you?" I giggled, looking over at my best friend, who'd already devoured her donut and had barely touched her sandwich.

"Never mind. I don't want to talk about him or think about him anymore. Just trust me when I say he isn't what he appears."

We sat there in silence for a few moments, each of us taking a bite of our sandwich. Then Lorelai looked over at me.

"What is it?" I questioned. "You look like you want to ask me something."

She picked up her pop and took a sip and then smiled at me.

"Well, I'm wondering if it would it bother you if I took the bedroom I originally wanted?" she asked quietly.

"I thought you didn't want it anymore?"

She shrugged. "I might have lied."

I shook my head. "You are unbelievable," I muttered.

"What?" she asked, laughing.

"Never mind."

____

Chapter 19

Dylan - Two Weeks Later

"WHEN DO you start your job again?" I asked, coming up behind Aurora and digging my fingers into her upper back, massaging her.

She closed her eyes and let out a tiny moan. "Uh, what day is it?" she muttered, getting lost in my touch.

"Wednesday," I said, pulling her back against me and kissing the side of her neck.

"Uh, I guess on Monday. That is if I ever finish packing everything," she said, opening her eyes and looking around at the last little bit that was left to pack. "Which is why I asked you over here, to help me." She turned enough so she could kiss my lips.

"Am I not helping?" I questioned, wrapping my arms around her and pulling her back against me before she walked away. I'd been helping up until Lorelai left ten minutes ago to go to the store for some drinks. Now that we were alone, my mind was on other things.

"Yeah, you are helping. Now, why were you wondering when I start?" she said, turning in my arms and running her fingers through my hair.

"Practices start on Monday, and I'll probably need some extra TLC." I winked. "Was hoping maybe I could book an appointment."

"Uh-huh," she said, kissing me.

"What? I'm only being honest here," I said as our lips parted.

"I'm sure you are." She giggled, her cheeks turning light pink. "I've got to get the next box packed. If Lorelai comes home and all I've gotten done is these two boxes, she'll beat me."

She pulled out of my arms just as I felt my phone vibrate in my pocket. I ignored that, going up to where Aurora stood wrapping some things and placing them in a box. I wrapped my arms around her again and kissed the side of her neck, moving to her shoulder.

"Why are you buzzing?" Aurora asked, giggling.

"You can feel that too?" I asked, raising my brows at her. "I thought it was just me."

She shook her head. "You are impossible." She laughed as she pulled away from me to grab some more items. "Just answer it."

I pulled my phone from my pocket. "Hello."

"Dylan, it's Thomas. Are you able to meet me at the arena in an hour?"

"Uh, can we make it an hour and thirty?" I questioned. "Possibly longer?" I said, looking at my watch, trying to remember what time the ferry would be here.

Aurora looked up at me, questions in her eyes as I listened, and finally hung up.

"You are in luck," I said, pulling her into me. "You've been saved, thanks to the vibration in my pants." I chuckled. "I have to go."

"Where?"

"Thomas wants to see me."

Aurora looked around the apartment and let out a sigh just as the front door opened and Lorelai walked in.

"I'll see you girls in the morning at the new condo," I said, grabbing my coat from the hook just inside the door.

"Leaving already?" Lorelai cried. "I just got the drinks." She pouted, not knowing what was going on.

"Dylan has a meeting to attend, so it's just you and me. We've got this."

I walked over, pressed a kiss to her lips, and made

my way out the door. I couldn't wait to get this meeting over with.

"YOU JUST ABOUT ready to turn the lights off?" Aurora murmured.

She'd been almost asleep on my chest for half an hour, but I wanted to see the news.

We were spending the night in her new place. I had Clay, Lucas, Knox, and Phil come by to help get the girls set up. We'd made significant progress getting things all set up, but by nine thirty, Aurora was falling asleep, her head on my lap while we were lying on the couch.

"Almost. I just want to see what they are putting out about me," I whispered, running my fingers gently up and down her arm. After my meeting with Thomas and the other lawyers for the Dominators, our public relations team wanted to do a press release. Relief had flooded me when he told me about the outcome of the tests. I didn't know why because I knew right from the start that the baby wasn't mine. It was more stressful than anything because it never failed. With terrible publicity came contract losses. Luckily, that hadn't happened this time.

"You were there," she muttered in the most adorable sleepy tone there was as she rubbed at her eyes.

I reached up and shut the bedside light off and relaxed back against my pillow, my arm behind my head.

"Thank you," Aurora said, lifting her head and placing a kiss on my lips.

I closed my eyes, taking her mouth. This right here was everywhere I wanted to be. With her, and nowhere else. My hands ran over her naked body, and I rolled her onto her back, my forearm supporting me. As our lips parted, I brushed the loose strands of hair back from her face and looked down into her eyes.

"I thought you wanted to watch the news?" she asked.

"Mmm, I may have found something a little more enticing," I said, meeting her lips again.

"Is that so? More enticing than seeing your name cleared?"

"Definitely more enticing," I whispered, sliding my free hand between her legs.

She let out a soft moan and covered my hand with hers as I gently rubbed her clit. I loved watching her expression as she lay there with her eyes closed while I pleasured her.

She parted her legs a bit more, allowing me a little more access. I slid two fingers deep inside of her as I bent down and met her lips. Her arms wrapped around me as our kiss deepened.

"That feels so good," she moaned.

"Do you want more?"

Her eyes met mine, and from the light of the TV, I could see she was flushed. She bit her bottom lip and nodded.

"What do you want?" I quietly asked.

"You," she whispered. I hissed as she took my cock in her hand, stroking me.

I pulled my fingers from inside her, rubbing her clit as I kissed. Reaching over, I opened her nightstand drawer, pulling a condom from the box. I was just about to rip it open when she put her hand on mine.

"No protection tonight," she said, looking up at me.

I ignored her request and had just ripped the packet open when she grabbed the condom from me.

"I mean it," she whispered.

"I don't know, I think we should…"

"We have. I want this. I want to feel you, all of you, right here." She brought hand down between her legs. Let's break in the new place while you break me in."

My already hardened cock throbbed as she met my eyes. I bent down and took her lips again. She placed her leg on my hip and brought her hand to my cheek.

"You're sure?" I asked.

She bit her bottom lip and nodded. "Make me yours."

I slid myself inside of her, wrapped my arms around her, and met her lips to quiet her moans.

"Go slow. I want to feel every inch of you."

Raising myself up on my elbow, I gripped her hip and thrust into her.

"Oh god, Dylan," she cried as I thrust a little harder and deeper.

My tongue washed through her mouth as I kissed her. With each thrust, she tightened around me as she dug her fingers into my back.

She wrapped her legs higher around my waist, running her fingers through my hair as she arched underneath me.

"God, Dylan, I'm so close," she said, sucking her bottom lip between her teeth.

"Let go, baby, whenever you're ready."

My tongue washed through her mouth as she wrapped her arms around me, digging her fingers into my back as I thrust myself into her at a faster pace. I could feel my orgasm building, my legs starting to feel numb when she finally let go. Seconds later, I followed, spilling into her.

I collapsed onto the bed beside her and pulled her against me. She rolled over onto her other side, facing away from me, as she wiggled her ass against me.

"Be careful there." I chuckled. "You'll get me going again."

She wiggled again against my cock and let out a tiny giggle. Almost immediately, I felt my cock hardening as I kissed the side of her neck and pulled her tighter against me. "I love you," I whispered between kisses.

"I love you too."

FIRST DAY of training was finally here, which meant today was Aurora's first day of work. I made my way down the hall toward her office, the smell of egg wraps making my stomach rumble. I'd stopped on my way to the arena and grabbed two spinach, ham and cheese egg wraps and a hot coffee for Aurora from Sip and Stir, since she'd messaged me on her way in complaining she'd overslept and hadn't had a chance to eat.

I raised my hand and knocked on the closed door that had her name plate on it.

"Come in," I heard her sleepy voice say.

I pushed the door open to see her sitting behind her desk, looking over some files. She didn't look up. Instead, she sat there, biting on the end of a pencil and twirling her hair around her finger.

"Someone call for breakfast?" I asked.

Finally, she ripped her eyes off the papers she was looking at and a smile immediately fell to her lips.

"What is this?" she asked, getting up from behind the desk and making her way over to me.

"Egg wrap and a coffee," I said, placing the bag down on her desk.

She walked over to me, placed her hands on my chest, and rose on her toes to kiss me. "You are a lifesaver."

"I try." I shrugged.

She dug into the bag and pulled one wrap out, handing it to me, before proceeding to unwrap hers and take a bite.

"God, this is good." She moaned.

"You're making me jealous. You didn't quite make that same sound the other night with me. Are you saying an egg wrap pleasures you more than I do?"

She let out an adorable laugh and shook her head. "Only when I'm literally starving."

"Thanks." I chuckled. "Which reminds me, I have to go, but I wanted to let you know I've made dinner reservations for Friday."

"Oh?"

"Yep, at The Sunset. I sent an invitation to Walker and your mom. Oh, and Lorelai. Thought we'd celebrate."

"Celebrate what?" she questioned, shoving the last of her egg wrap into her mouth.

"New job, new place, your brother's birthday, and us," I said, pulling her into my arms.

"Sounds perfect. I can't wait."

I heard commotion outside her door just as I leaned down to kiss her lips.

"Come on there, lover boy, the ice awaits," Knox said, popping his head into the room.

Aurora laughed as she hugged me tight. "Have fun."

"You too. Good luck."

I quickly kissed her cheek then pulled another bag from my pocket. She looked down a small smile on her lips.

"What is that?" She questioned, taking the bag from my hand and opening it up.

"A surprise." I winked.

I watched as her eyes lit up at the cinnamon scone

I'd ordered. "To calm the first day jitters." I said, placing a kiss on her cheek.

"Thank you!" She called as I took off after Knox leaving her in her office. .

Chapter 20

Dylan

"MR. HAYES, YOUR TABLE IS READY."

Dylan took hold of my hand and waited as the hostess grabbed six menus. We followed Walker, my mother, and Lorelai to the table.

"I got the best table in the place," he said, leaning in and whispering in my ear. "Tonight is a cause for a huge celebration." He winked.

"Dylan, this place is beautiful," Penelope said, turning and smiling at the pair of us. The smile I noticed barely reached her eyes. We'd gotten her settled into a small apartment a few days before we'd moved. She said she was happy there, but I knew she wasn't. I had never seen her take so long to heal after a breakup. She missed Joe, and we all knew it.

Dylan smiled. "When I brought Aurora last time, she'd raved about the food, so I figured we'd come back for tonight."

"Well, from the looks of it, it's a brilliant choice," she said, catching up to Walker and Lorelai.

Once we were at the table, we all took a seat at the table, and everyone opened the menu while Dylan ordered two bottles of the same wine I'd had that night we'd first come here.

He took hold of my hand and softly smiled at me. I knew he felt bad that he'd not been able to be with me the night of graduation and insisted he make it up to me. However, he'd more than made it up to me over the last few weeks, but he still insisted on celebrating.

"My goodness, everything looks so good. I don't know what to order," Lorelai said, leaning into me.

"I'm going to go with the lasagna. I wanted to order it the last time, but you know me and salmon. I had to go with that instead." I giggled.

"I swear you have had salmon in every restaurant we've been to in Victoria and Vancouver." Lorelai giggled. "Time you spread your wings." She winked.

"Oh, that sounds good," my mother said, still looking over the options.

"Salmon or lasagna?" I questioned.

"Lasagna. Salmon is, well, not my favourite."

"What about you, Walker?" Dylan asked.

"Definitely the surf and turf," he answered. "I checked the menu out online when you messaged me. I've been craving it since."

"My kind of guy," Dylan replied, patting him on the shoulder. "I think I'm going to have the same."

Dylan rested his hand on my upper thigh and picked up his wineglass. "Guys, I'd like to take a minute while we are all trying to decide what to eat to congratulate Aurora and Lorelai on their graduation."

Everyone picked up their glass, and we all clinked glasses together and took a drink.

"And to their new positions with the Dominators."

Again, we all clinked glasses and took another drink.

"How does it feel to be working with them?" my mother questioned.

Lorelai glanced over at me and smiled. "For me, it almost feels surreal that we are actually not in school anymore and we are working, but I am very excited about the future."

"Me too. It was a long road, and I am so glad we are finished. Now, it's on to better things." I smiled, meeting Dylan's eyes. "Oh, and we can't forget, happy birthday to my brother, Walker," I said, smiling over at him.

"Yeah, Happy Birthday," Lorelai added.

"Thanks," Walker said, making eye contact with her.

Lorelai cleared her throat and pushed her chair back from the table. "Please excuse me, I just need to use the little girl's room."

For the first time, she smiled at Walker without tears in her eyes. Perhaps she was finally over what had happened between them. At least, I hoped she was.

Mom stood as well. "Lorelai, I think I'll join you."

They both took off toward the washroom, leaving the three of us at the table.

"Who's the empty seat and extra menu for?" I questioned, taking a drink of my wine.

Almost as if on cue, Dylan stood up and waved. I glanced over my shoulder to see Knox coming toward the table. He smiled in my direction and grabbed the seat beside Walker.

"Oh my god, Knox Evans…this can't be real," Walker said, a look of shock and surprise on his face.

I couldn't help but smile. Walker still hadn't gotten over meeting Dylan, and Knox was his second favorite player. I glanced over at Dylan and then immediately thought of Lorelai, panic mode already beginning to set in.

"In the flesh," Knox said, shaking hands with Walker. "Dylan told me you are a huge fan."

"Never miss a game," he said, looking proudly.

"We love fans that like, don't we, Dylan."

"Absolutely. If only I could get my girl here to be that dedicated," he said, winking at me.

"I'm dedicated," I said, sticking my tongue out at him, then laughing. Once the new season started, I'd promised I'd get better.

"You better be." Dylan leaned over and placed a kiss on my lips. That was when I heard the gasp. I glanced up to see Lorelai standing there, glaring at me.

"What's wrong?" I questioned, still smiling.

"What is he doing here?" Lorelai said, glancing toward Knox, not hiding her displeasure at all.

"Hey, Lorelai, love your face," Knox said, winking at her.

Trying to divert a disaster in the making, I got up and grabbed hold of Lorelai's hand and pulled her through the restaurant and out to the entrance.

"Just for tonight, give this man a break," I said, crossing my arms in front of me. "He's done a lot for us in the last couple of weeks. Tomorrow, you can go back to your hatred for him. Just don't ruin tonight," I pleaded.

"He's done a lot for you. For me, he only made move-in day that much harder when he'd had all my bedroom furniture delivered to the wrong bedroom."

"Whose fault would that be?"

Lorelai let out a huff. "Fine, if I must endure this man tonight, then bring on the wine."

"You better get over whatever it is he's done, because in about two weeks you may need to treat him for an injury, and then what will happen?"

Lorelai straightened and then turned and looked at me. "If that were to happen, I guess I'd have to be professional. Until then, it is what it is." She turned and walked back toward the table, holding her head high.

AFTER DINNER, Dylan, Walker, and Knox excused themselves and headed outside to the parking lot, leaving Lorelai, my mom, and me at the table. Knox had brought a couple signed jerseys for my brother for his birthday, and they wanted to give them to him before Knox had to leave for the night.

I sipped on my wine and sat back in my chair. "Mom, are you sure you're going to be happy in this new place you've found?" I questioned.

I'd really wanted to see her try to work things out with Joe before grabbing her own place, but she'd been insistent.

"Oh, it's perfect for me. To be honest, I was looking for someplace a bit smaller." She smiled.

"Mom, why didn't you try and work things out with Joe?"

My mom sat back in her seat and thought for a moment. Then she looked at me. "Aurora, I hope you'll never be in a position to understand this. When I found out Joe was against your relationship with Dylan, it bothered me. The fact that he wouldn't want to see his own son be happy really upset me. No matter what I told him, he didn't seem to care. He was so against it, he told me he'd disown his own son before he'd accept your relationship, and he told me I was foolish if I wouldn't do the same."

I looked over at Lorelai, who sat there with the same shocked expression on her face as I did. I wasn't sure what to make of it. I wasn't even sure if Dylan knew his father had said those things, because I knew neither of us cared enough to talk about it. We were who we were, and I knew without a doubt in my mind that he was who I wanted to be with, no matter what.

"To be honest with you, I have been trying to search within myself to find a way to make up for all those years of being a terrible mother."

"You weren't a terrible mother," I answered.

"Oh, honey, no, I was bad. You had very little guidance, and I'm grateful you turned out to be as good as you are. So, this was how I could do it, how I felt I could make up all those years of not being there to you. I let him go. I don't want to be with a man who would spit in the face of love that way. If he does that to others, what will he do to us in five or ten years. Plus, and I'm being honest here, he was a little too controlling for my liking. You know me, I'm a free spirit."

My vision became a little blurry. I wasn't sure why. My mother had never made me cry before.

"I just, I thought you were finally happy," I said, wiping at my eyes.

"I was for a while. However, your happiness means so much more to me than my own does."

I wiped at my eyes again and took a sip of my wine to help clear the tightness in my throat. I never thought my mother cared that much about me to give up something she wanted.

"Plus, if I'm being honest with myself, I'm a dreamer, Aurora, and you and Dylan have the fairy tale. I wanted that for myself, but he certainly wasn't my prince charming. So if you two are lucky to have that, I want to make sure it stays that way. I see the way he looks at you, and you at him. You two are so in sync with one another, it's frightening to me. I can't even remember what that feels like anymore.

"You mean you had that once before?" I asked.

My mother nodded. "That was what it was like with your father, and I've never been able to find that again."

She looked at me and smiled through the tears in her eyes. "And to answer your question, what you have with Dylan is definitely love. Never mistake it for anything but and, my dear, wrap your arms around it and never let it go."

All this time, I'd never realized how much my mother actually loved me until tonight.

"Oh god, that was so beautiful, Penelope," Lorelai cried, wiping the tears from her cheeks. "Maybe one day I'll find that kind of love." She sniffled and picked up her seventh glass of wine and drank it down.

I couldn't help but laugh at Lorelai and her flushed cheeks. I couldn't remember the last time she'd drank so much, and it was all because Knox had joined us for dinner. I wrapped my arm around Lorelai and pulled her close. "You'll have it one day," I said. "Probably with someone you hate." I winked, glancing across to the spot where Knox had been sitting.

"I swear, Aurora, don't start," she said, getting a little red in the face.

Mom and I burst out laughing, and soon she was laughing too.

WE ORDERED dessert once Walker and Knox left. Lorelai seemed to be more at ease and was finally smiling again. Dylan quickly took care of the tab, and we made our way out to the parking lot.

"Thank you so much for dinner," my mother said, turning toward me and Dylan.

"My pleasure. These two ladies have worked hard." He pulled me against him and placed a kiss on my forehead.

"That they have. I'm very proud of the pair of them." She winked.

"Are you coming home?" Lorelai asked, turning toward me.

I was about to say yes, but Dylan spoke up first. "If it's okay with you, I'd like to monopolize her for one more night. I'll have her home first thing in the morning, and I'll even help with more unpacking." He added.

"Eight sharp," Lorelai said, smiling.

I wasn't sure if she was kidding or not. "Eight sharp?" I repeated. "It's Saturday."

"Wimps. Fine, how is ten? This guy doesn't like to get up too early on his days off." Dylan chuckled.

"Honestly," Lorelai said, shaking her head.

The four of us laughed. "Ten is fine." She winked, pulling me in for a hug.

We watched as Mom and Lorelai climbed into the car and pulled away, then Dylan pulled me into his side and turned toward his car.

"So, you want me all to yourself, hmmm?"

"I do. There will be lots of nights you'll spend alone soon enough. I want to make the most of the time we have together, otherwise I'll be on one end of the phone or camera and you on the other, and while that is fun, this is better."

My heart skipped a beat hearing those words leave his mouth. I hoped this phase of our relationship would last forever.

WE WALKED hand-in-hand through the park across the street from Dylan's condo. It was a quiet night. Few people were out, despite the gorgeous weather. He stopped at a park bench and sat down, pulling me down beside him.

"You have a good time tonight?" he asked.

"I did. Best time. Thank you for everything tonight."

He placed his hand on my cheek and leaned in, placing his lips on mine. "You're welcome," he whispered as our lips parted.

He placed his arm on the back of the bench, and I cuddled into his side, and we sat there staring out at the water.

"I've been doing a lot of thinking over the past little while."

"Oh?"

"I know you haven't said anything to Lorelai about moving in with me."

Dylan had asked me a couple weeks before Lorelai and I signed the lease about moving in with him. I hadn't answered him then because it was more about the timing of the situation, but now I was starting to feel a little worried that he thought maybe I didn't want to move in with him.

"Dylan, I can explain."

"No need. I know you probably didn't want to mention anything because of the whole job thing, and rent here is expensive, and I know you love Lorelai like a sister."

"I do," I replied.

"So, with me being gone all the time, I'd rather know you are with her than on your own in my place, even though you're perfectly safe there. So, how about we agree that when I'm home, you'll stay with me, but when I'm on the road, you'll stay with Lorelai."

Almost immediately, that defensiveness I was feeling floated away, and I realized Dylan was more than okay with that arrangement. I hadn't even had to say it.

"I think that is a great idea," I said.

"We can wait and talk more about moving in together later."

I nodded. "I'd like that."

I rested my head on his shoulder, and he wrapped his arm around me, taking my free hand in his. We sat there together quietly, just enjoying one another's company. I knew in him I'd found my forever, and I couldn't be more excited to start that journey with him by my side.

GET A FREE BOOK

Sign up for my newsletter and I'll send you a free book.

https://geni.us/NLSignupBackMatter

What is coming next from S.L. Sterling

Ten Minute Misconduct (Vancouver Dominators # 2)
July 23rd
Preorder Here: https://geni.us/TenMinuteMisconduct

Summer Nights and Fireflies
Coming Soon
Preorder Here: https://geni.us/SummerNightsFireflies

The Christmas Card (Willow Valley)
December 2024
https://geni.us/TheChristmasCardWV6

ACE (Vegas MMA)
January 2025
https://geni.us/AceVegasMMA

Follow S.L. Sterling

Did you know that bookbub has a feature where you can follow me and it will send you an alert when I release a book or put a title on sale? Sign up here and make sure you stay in the loop.

Bookbub:
https://geni.us/SLSterlingBookbub

Website
https://www.authorslsterling.com

Facebook
https://geni.us/SLSterlingFB

Twitter
https://geni.us/SLSterlingTwitter

Instagram
https://geni.us/SLSterlingInstagram

Tiktok
https://geni.us/slsterlingtiktok

Reader Group

Follow Me

https://geni.us/SapphiresReaderGroup

Goodreads
https://geni.us/SterlingGoodreads

Newsletter
https://geni.us/NLSignupBackMatter

About the Author

USA Today Bestselling Author S.L. Sterling was born and raised in southern Ontario. She now lives in Northern Ontario Canada and is married to her best friend and soul mate and their two dogs.

An avid reader all her life, S.L. Sterling dreamt of becoming an author. She decided to give writing a try after one of her favorite authors launched a course on how to write your novel. This course gave her the push she needed to put pen to paper and her debut novel "It Was Always You" was born.

When S.L. Sterling isn't writing or plotting her next novel she can be found curled up with a cup of coffee, blanket and the newest romance novel from one of her favorite authors.

In her spare time, she enjoys camping, hiking, sunny destinations, spending quality time with family and friends and of course reading.

To be notified of new releases or sales, join S.L.
Sterling's private Mailing List.
https://geni.us/NLSignupBackMatter

Get even more of the inside scoop when you join S.L.
Sterling's private Facebook group, Sterling's Silver
Sapphires: https://geni.us/SapphiresReaderGroup

It Was Always You

On A Silent Night

Bad Company

Back to You this Christmas

Fireside Love

Holiday Wishes

Saviour Boy

The Boy Under the Gazebo

The Greatest Gift

Into the Sunset

Letting You Go

The Spencer Brooks Diaries

Our Little Secret

Our Little Surprise

Our Little Wedding

The Malone Brother Series

A Kiss Beneath the Stars

In Your Arms

His to Hold

Finding Forever with You

Vegas MMA

Dagger

Doctors of Eastport General

Doctor Desire

Doctor Right

All I Want for Christmas (Contemporary Romance Holiday Collection)

Willow Valley

Memories of the Past

The Holiday Dilemma

Letters from the Heart

My Darling Christmas

Scars on my Heart

The Happy Holidates Series

Pop Tarts and Mistletoe

Champagne and Fireworks

Summer Nights and Fireflies

Vancouver Dominators

Inside the Penalty Box

Ten Minute Misconduct

www.ingramcontent.com/pod-product-compliance
Lightning Source LLC
Chambersburg PA
CBHW022105310726
48972CB00007B/1891